STITCH X FOR MURDER

STITCHES IN CRIME - BOOK 5

ACF BOOKENS

1

It was still hot as hades and muggier than hot cocoa outside, but I could see the promise of my favorite season coming to Octonia. The flowers were tipping toward the golden yellow that marked the autumn, and the sunlight lit up the house more fully because of its lower place in the sky. The temperature was still soaring, but I took hope in the fact that I was removing the spent tomatoes and cucumber vines from the garden and watching the cornstalks dry in the beds. I was going to be able to get mums and hang cornstalks for the new store-front soon.

As I gathered the last of the yellow cherry tomatoes before composting the vines, I planned out my autumn decorating plan for both shop and house. Cornstalks for the front of both structures. Mums in pots at both, too, to be planted over tulip bulbs that I hoped would survive the deer onslaught next spring. Two splendid eucalyptus and dried flower wreaths that I'd picked up at the city market last week. I was ready.

Indoor decorations would be much simpler – the autumn kitchen towels would come out, and I'd light some apple-scented candles. Beyond that, I didn't have much time or will. I was too eager to get the store open and running. Paisley's Architectural Salvage, my new shop at my friend Saul's construction yard, was set to open on Labor Day weekend, and I was buried in tasks big and small.

Fortunately, I had some great friends who had helped me get all the big pieces in place. It's amazing what three determined women and some big equipment can do. We had a lean-to built on my shed-shop, and the mantels and larger doors I had were safe and dry on display there. Inside, we'd used rough reclaimed boards to build open shelves, and I displayed samples of the moldings, corbels, and hardware I had available amongst my friend Mika's hand-made sweaters, socks, and mittens. The color of her knitted work against the grays and browns of the salvaged items made the space interesting and inviting. At least I thought so.

Today, though, I was at the shop simply to gather my tools from the storage room at the back, where I now kept them since a certain three-year-old had decided he'd be like Mommy and try to use a crowbar to remove our very-much-in-use baseboards in our house, and then head over to our new job site.

I jumped into my Subaru and tried to ignore the dust and mud caked into everything, including Sawyer's car seat, and headed north to town to pick up Mika. Our worksite today was an icon of Octonia County, out west of town deep in the Blue Ridge Mountains, and I didn't take for granted at all that I was the one who had been chosen to responsibly take it down.

The octagonal barn had been standing in a beautiful hollow nestled between two ancient mountains, and as best I could tell from public records and local legend, it had stood since the county was formed more than a hundred and fifty years ago. It was built as a grist mill where horses turned the stones to grind the corn that grew around it, and then it had become hay storage and then a cattle shed. Now, it was simply falling down, even though it had outlasted the farmhouse that had stood behind it by about twenty years.

The building was clad in gorgeous gray barn boards that were mostly in good shape, and I hoped to salvage a lot of those. But the treasure of the barn was inside – eight huge heart pine beams spanned from a central pillar and held up the rapidly failing roof. Each of the beams had been crafted from a single timber and measured about sixteen inches square. They were works of tremendous skill that needed to be saved, and I already had a timber frame company eager to buy the lot for a new project they were building up on the mountainside above town. But only if I could salvage all eight beams and the sixteen-foot pillar in the middle.

I'd been out to check the site with my son Sawyer a week earlier, and from what I could see, everything looked solid and free of insects. But the barn was a mess. Critters had been living there for a while, and the rafters were full of swallows' nests. The floor was covered in scat from raccoons and possums, and a very resourceful groundhog had undermined most of the supporting boards at the walls. It was going to be a tricky take-down, and while Sawyer very much wanted to join us that day, I had asked his grandparents to watch him so that he didn't get hurt or, more likely, injure us all by knocking out a crucial support beam with his "big muscles."

Instead, my best friend, Mika, had left her shop in the capable hands of her assistant, Mrs. Stephenson, and she was waiting at the curb for me to pick her up. My boyfriend, Santiago, had also taken the day off from his position as sheriff and was meeting us there with a couple of friends, and of course, Mika's uncle Saul would be there with his crew to run the equipment and haul away our takings. My job was simply to oversee things, identify the pieces we were taking and what would need to be burned or hauled away, and generally keep things on track.

Easier said than done with a team made up of an interesting mix of total novices and highly trained experts. I just hoped my very wonderful and very headstrong friends who were used to being in charge could actually take direction. If not, they might end up being escorted out of the hollow in the bucket of an excavator. Saul didn't take kindly to fools on his job sites, and while it was my job, it was most definitely his job site.

"I'm so excited," Mika said as she dropped into the bucket seat next to me wearing overalls, a tank top, and a super cute tie-dyed bandana over her long dark hair. She always looked ready for whatever was coming.

I, however, was in jeans with far too many holes in them to be fashionable, a tank top that no longer fit given how much my body had changed since I started doing all this physical work, and a bandana that rivaled my jeans in hole count. Underneath, my hair was unwashed, and while I had applied deodorant this morning, I did not smell what I would call my best. I didn't care, though. It was a work day, and I was excited. "Me, too," I said glancing over at Mika. "It's going to be a great day."

We chatted the rest of the way out of town and, as we climbed in elevation, I watched for signs that the trees were going to start putting on their leaf show. Nothing colorful was visible yet, but when your dad loves trees as much as mine does, you start to notice more subtle clues, like the way the trees were shedding their excess green to help them compensate for the late-season drought we'd been having. They were simply holding on until October when they could do their thing and then rest. I could relate.

As we pulled into the jobsite, I could see Saul's crew milling around with their usual thermoses and donuts, and Santiago and the two men he had brought along were right in the gaggle. I hadn't met Dom or Chris, but I had heard Santiago talk about them enough to feel like I had. They'd been friends since college, and when Santiago had come back home to begin his career as a police officer, the other two had found jobs in nearby Charlottesville because the three wanted to be near each other. Dom was an attorney who specialized in civil rights cases and worked for the local Legal Aid office in town, and Chris had just opened a really great food truck that made the most amazing gourmet mac and cheese I had ever eaten. It was called "Big Daddy Mac," and it already had quite the following as evidenced by the posts about it on social media.

I had told Mika that Dom and Chris would be here, but I hadn't mentioned that Chris was single and, from the pictures I'd seen from Santiago's day trips with them, very attractive with long dark hair, a couple shoulders' worth of tattoos, and a smile that was quite electric. I was hoping maybe they'd just hit it off . . . but I knew my friend too well to try to force anything. Proximity and hard work were going to have to do the match-making today.

I did take a tiny bit of hope, though, when she gave him a long look as we walked over. She was definitely intrigued.

But I didn't even have time to take count of my own romance beyond a quick arm squeeze as I walked by Santiago because Saul was already saddled up on the forklift and ready to go. I couldn't see his knees in the cab, but I imagined he was tapping his foot in impatience. Saul was a good man, but waiting was not something he enjoyed. At all.

I swung my hand around in a circle that I hoped showed I wanted everyone to gather around, and then I pulled out my notes. As Santiago and Mika rallied the troops, I started listing what we were trying to save, starting with the ceiling beams and central pillar. "I already have a customer for those, so they need to be our top priority. Everything else is bonus, understood?" I was doing my best impression of my fifth grade teacher, Mrs. Mackey, who could command a room with a single syllable despite the fact that she was under five feet tall, and it seemed to be working. All eyes were on me.

"Mika, you and Chris are working with Saul to get the roof off first thing. Head on over. He's ready," I said and hoped I seemed casual with my pairing there.

"Santiago, you are guiding our bulldozer and skid steer guys as they clear the perimeter for us. We have permission to push back twenty feet beyond the building so we can move around more easily." Santiago nodded and followed the two members of Saul's crew who headed right for their machines.

"Dom, you and I are going to be in charge of pulling down barn boards with the help of you guys," I pointed to the last two members of Saul's crew, "who are loading the truck. Work for you?" When all three men nodded, we headed over to stage the scaffolding that we would set up as soon as Saul got the roof off.

From the looks of things, that was going to be quick work since he was able to lift it in two big pieces. Apparently, it hadn't been in terrible shape, aside from the gaping holes, and I thought maybe we could claim some of the lathing below the existing metal so that Dad could make some more picture frames for my shop.

That could wait, though. We had to get to those beams, so as soon as Saul moved out of the way, I recruited Mika and Chris to our team, strategically placing them on the same piece of scaffold after we got it set up, and started taking down the barn boards. Most of them were still really solid, and the ones that crumbled totally disintegrated, so we didn't even have that much waste to contend with.

When Santiago and his work crew finished clearing, they set up the final scaffold set and began helping us take down the boards while Saul circled us and let us load the boards onto his forks to be distributed to the truck. It wasn't a speedy process since the boards all had to be pried off individually, but eventually, we got the building defaced – loved this positive turn on a word associated with vandalism most of the time – and it was just time for lunch.

Just at that moment, The Mac Daddy truck pulled into the lot, and a very beautiful young woman jumped out of the cab. "Anyone hungry?" she asked before giving Chris a very long, tight hug. I know I wasn't imagining it when I saw Mika's face fall.

"Everyone, meet my daughter, Jill," Chris said, and I snuck just enough of a peek at Mika to see she was smiling again. "She runs the truck with me, and we thought you might all like a little mac today. We even have vegan macaroni and cheese."

"Blasphemy," Saul said with a smile as he put himself first in line. "What do you have with bacon?"

While everyone else queued up for food, Santiago and I perched on the hood of my car to chat. "Lots of progress this morning," he said as he took my hand in his. "You pleased?"

I nodded. "Yeah, I am. The boards will sell well, maybe even as a lot." I stared at the skeleton of the barn standing there like a canvas-less circus tent. "But I'll feel a lot better when we get the beams down. I hate to disappoint my customer if they aren't any good."

Mika handed me a bowl as she sat down next to me. "Mushroom Mac – thought you might like it," she said.

Behind us, Dom and Chris leaned against the sides of my car, bowls of their own cheesy goodness in hand after Chris gave Santiago a bowl that looked to be full of some sort of delicious looking sausage. "It's a hot one, Santi," he said.

"Good," Santiago answered. "Nothing like heat to cool you down on a day like today."

I shook my head at his logic and bit into my own food. It was amazing – creamy and rich, and the mushrooms added an earthy goodness that made me feel like I was sitting by a bonfire on a fall evening. "Oh my word, Chris," I said. "This is the best thing I've ever tasted."

He laughed. "Thank you. That's Jill's recipe. She eats a mostly plant-based diet and is always looking for ways to incorporate more veggies. I'll let her know you liked it."

"Please do," I said with my mouth entirely full.

Silence settled around us like a gentle rain as we ate, and by the time all the crew had finished their meals and disposed of the compostable bowls that Chris and Jill used, we were all quiet and satiated. "Let's do this," I said.

The men and Mika moved to the stations I assigned them, and soon Saul and his crew were using the forklift and the skid steer to gently lift the first of the beams off the center pillar. As they brought it down in front of me, I walked its length and found it was in perfect condition. Not a bit of insect or water damage in sight. "We're good," I said, and a small cheer went up from the group as the men drove the beam over to the back end of the flatbed we had already loaded with barn boards.

The rest of the afternoon moved right along, and when we were done, we had a solid central pillar and eight great beams for my client. It was going to be a good month for the business, and I was hoping that would mean I could put aside some cash for improvements at the farmhouse as well as sock some extra into my retirement and Sawyer's college fund.

As the crew loaded their machines back on their trailers and packed up the scaffolding in Saul's truck, Santiago, Dom, Chris, Mika, and I did one last walk around the site. The barn had long ago been gutted, so we didn't have any more wood or fixtures to salvage from inside, but in old buildings with dirt floors, lots of things were buried, and I was hopeful we might find some old bottles or even farm equipment like pulleys or hay hooks for the shop.

As we spread out around what had been the interior of the barn, we kicked our feet and stirred up clouds of dust that would make us each look a little like Sawyer did at the end of each day, dirt-covered and delighted. Santiago unearthed a small trove of bottles in what looked like it might have been a privy site at some point, and we began loading the crates I carried in my car with blue, brown, and clear glass from a variety of ointments, tinctures, and booze. Most of the blue glass would go to my house for my personal collection, but the other bottles would make a great display in the shop.

While privy holes were a little psychologically gross to dig into, they were also often rich with old stuff because back in the day, people didn't take things to the dump. They just buried things in the yard, and if you already had a hole dug for your bathroom, why not use it as a place to get rid of the other stuff you didn't need? Plus, by now, the bathroom contributions had long since decomposed, so we were just left with a bunch of precious trash that had been used to fill up the hole long after the facilities were in use.

It was a good thing we had gotten the building down quickly because this was one deep privy hole, and after an hour of pulling every manner of bottle, ceramics, and even a dented, but intact, pewter cup out of the hole, we were nowhere near the bottom. Mika had volunteered to go in, and she was now waist-deep in the hole and bringing up more and more as she sank further and further into the ground.

It wasn't labor intensive work, and the five of us were laughing and enjoying our finds, so I didn't think anybody minded a little dirty labor on a Friday afternoon. We were wondering exactly what someone would use "peppermint tonic" for when a woman said, "Ah, privy digging. My favorite."

I looked up to see Summer Ross standing over us and smiling. Summer owned the property the barn had stood on, and she'd sold the salvage job to me specifically because she wanted to see the materials used responsibly. She was an environmental activist and had actually spent days in trees to protect both redwoods and owls in the not-too-distant past. Now, though, she had turned her efforts to protecting the natural elements of Octonia, her new home. She'd bought an old plantation house up the road from where we were and had spent, reportedly, millions to take the house back to some of its original grandeur but also to get it LEED Platinum certified. She was kind of my hero.

"We've found some really good stuff. Want any of it?" I asked. Technically, everything was mine since I'd bought the rights but I definitely didn't want to be stingy with things that didn't cost me anything extra to get. Plus, I knew she'd appreciate the finds.

Summer knelt by the crates and carefully looked through the bottles and ceramic. She took out a small brown bottle with a red stopper still intact. "This will be perfect for my collection of small things. Thanks, Paisley," she said.

As she looked around her, she smiled. "When you say you'll leave the place pristine, you really mean it, don't you?"

"I try my best," I said as I stood up next to her. "I know you're going to be turning this into pasture, and I didn't want any of the animals to get hurt by leftover nails or," I pointed to the crates, "broken glass. Look okay?"

"I'll be moving the alpacas in tomorrow if the fencers can come. It looks perfect. Thank you." She smiled again as she looked down at Mika and the men who were still hauling out goodies. "You guys have fun."

As she turned to go, Mika squawked like a chicken and said, "I think the fun part is over." In her hand, she held up a human skull.

2

"Oh Lordie," Summer said as she sat down hard on the ground beside me. "It wasn't just a story."

Santiago was already on the phone and calling in Deputy Winslow to help secure the scene. I could hear the tone of his voice, and he was in official sheriff mode now. I sat down with Summer and asked, "What do you mean?

She shook her head and pulled her eyes away from the skull, which Mika had set gently on the ground beside the privy hole. We weren't going anywhere with anything we'd retrieved just yet.

When Summer met my eyes, she said, "I thought it was just talk, just folks not wanting things to change. You know how folks around here can be."

I did know. Many people in our beautiful rural county really wanted things to go backwards instead of forwards. That was true for buildings but also for things like LGBTQ+ rights and access for disabled people. Sometimes it felt like our county motto was, "Even if it was broke, don't fix it."

"Two old-timers came back last week and told me that I had better leave the barn as it was, let it fall down on itself. 'Nothing

good will come out of digging up the past,' one of them said."
Her eyes grew wide. "They knew."

I put my hand on her arm. "Maybe. Or maybe not. It could
just be that they were sad and didn't want the barn to get taken
down. You need to tell Santiago, though."

She nodded, and as she took some deep breaths and closed
her eyes, I signaled for Santi to come over when he was done
with his call. He nodded, and I turned back to Summer. She
was still quietly breathing, and it looked like she needed to
focus her attention there.

I stood up, dusted off the backside of my pants, and walked
back over to Mika, Dom, and Chris. "You okay?" I said to Mika
as I hugged her.

"Seriously, Paisley, why do we find all the bodies? Are there
so many secrets around here that we can't help but dig them
up?" She ran her fingers through her hair and then squeaked.
"Anyone have any hand sanitizer?"

Chris reached into his pocket and handed her a small
bottle. "Always," he said.

Mika lathered up her hands, gave the bottle back to Chris,
and then shook her hands until they were dry. "Thanks," she
said, "but really, Paisley?"

Dom sighed. "Maybe everyone finds bodies around here,
but you two are the only responsible ones to report the finds."
He shrugged.

"I'm not sure it makes me feel better to think that there are
a bunch of unreported murders in my town, but thanks," Mika
said with a wan smile.

I put my arm around my friend's shoulder and squeezed
her close. "We dig up things, Mika. That's my job. But I'm sorry
you keep getting dragged into these horrible finds."

Mika swallowed. "What are you sorry for? You didn't kill
these people. And I wouldn't want you out here by yourself

finding a skull, you know." She gave me a look of part anger, part sympathy. "We're in this together."

"Always," I said. "You guys okay?" I turned to the two men who were sitting on the ground.

"Oh yeah. I'm just reliving my days as MacBeth in college." Chris said as he laid a hand on the center of his chest.

"No, we're not going Shakespeare in the, um, field," Dom said. "No 'Alas' here, okay?"

Chris rolled his eyes. "Spoilsport. But seriously, that is sad. Someone has been buried in an outhouse hole for who knows how long." His face got a shade paler, and Mika moved to sit next to him.

Even in this moment of awfulness, I couldn't help but feel a little lift of joy that these two had, at least, become friendly. I smiled as she put her hand on his shoulder and squeezed.

Apparently, Dom was of the same mindset because he caught my eye and winked just as Santiago and Summer came over. "Winslow is on her way," Santiago said as he slipped his arm around my waist. "Sadly, I think you two know the drill," he said to Mika and me. "I need you to hang around until she can get your statements."

"Us, too, I suppose," Chris said.

"Yep, you, too. But I promise after we get squared here, we'll all go for burgers," Santiago said. "My treat."

"Now, let's be clear here," Chris said. "When you say 'my treat' we aren't talking slabs of frozen beef on flat buns from a drive-thru, are we? We're past that stage in our friendship, I believe, and I cannot accept such a gift."

"We have the best burgers in the state, I'll have you know," Santiago said as he looked at me. "Back me up, Pais?"

"He's right, but just because we have them doesn't mean that's where you're taking us all for dinner," I said with a wink.

Dom laughed. "I like her," he said. "And she has a point."

"Burgers and beer on me at the Lafayette Inn after we finish here," Santiago said very slowly. "Clear enough for you?"

"Crystal," Chris said. "Now what?"

"Well," Santiago said hesitantly, "If you guys are up for it, we need to see if there are more remains."

Mika stood up. "Tell me how to do it, and I'll go back in. No one, not even a skeleton, deserves to be left this way."

Chris stood up. "I like you, Mika Grace," he said with a smile. "I'll be your right-hand man."

Dom, Santiago, and I all exchanged a look, and Summer grinned and said, "Well, those two have that handled. What else can we do?" She clearly understood the situation and was savvily suggesting we give these two some time alone.

"Since this is now a crime scene, we need to scour the site for other evidence." He sighed. "This may be mostly pointless given that most of the site just left on a truck, but we should still check."

"And then we'll need to check at Saul's lot, too, look at the materials we gathered?" I asked.

"Yep, but as long as Saul agrees to Winslow's conditions – she's stopping there on her way here – that can wait until tomorrow," Santiago said. "He'll tarp everything and let his crew know to leave it be."

"I'm sure he will," I said. "So coach us on what to look for?"

"Wish I could tell you," Santiago said. "Until we know cause of death, I can't tell you what the weapon might be. So we look for anything that could have been a weapon."

"Bullets, bats, poison," Summer said and then turned to look at the crates of bottles nearby. "Guess that might be a starting place?"

"Yep. I'll need to take all of those in and have them checked," Santiago said. "Let's spread out."

The three of us headed in different directions and walked carefully as we stared at the ground. I had done this twice before already, and I had a pocketful of nails to show for it but nothing else. I didn't think it likely we would find anything at all, but I wanted to be thorough so I kept scouring.

Just as I was about to say it was hopeless, Mika hollered. "You can stop looking. I found the murder weapon." In her hand, she held a huge knife, and from the looks of the blade, the dried blood of our skeleton was still on it.

Chris helped Mika out of the hole, and Santiago carefully took the knife in his gloved hand and then slipped it into an evidence bag. "You didn't get cut, did you?" he asked Mika.

"Nope. Chris gave me these fireproof gloves, and they protected my hand." She smiled at Chris, who blushed. "You think that could be what killed this poor person?"

Santiago turned the knife over in his hands. "That sure looks like blood to me, but we won't know until we test it, of course."

Mika nodded. "I think I'm almost at the bottom, but maybe someone who knows anatomy better than Chris could help him out." She gestured toward the pile of bones that I had completely missed in the excitement of the knife find.

"Whoa," I said. "So someone did throw an entire body in the privy?"

"Sure looks like it," Chris said as he arranged what I thought was an arm bone down by the kneecap.

"Let me help," Summer said and quickly began arranging the bones in what actually resembled a skeleton, or at least the skeleton that had hung in my high school biology classroom. "I was a nurse before I retired."

Chris smiled. "You're retired? You can't be a day over forty."

"Forty-two actually, and thank you. Unfortunately, my husband died young, but he left me enough money to live on for the rest of my life . . . and while I loved nursing, I felt a real calling to do something else. Hence, this farm."

"And all the activism . . ." I said. "Summer used to volunteer with Greenpeace and The Sierra Club." I didn't know this woman too well, but she, like many a woman I knew, often downplayed her work, especially to men. I wasn't about to let that happen. "She's an environmental powerhouse."

"Wow," Dom said. "Maybe when we're not trying to solve a murder, you can consult with me on a case I have in Charlottesville?"

She smiled and blushed. "I'd like that."

Santiago, Chris, and I smirked and looked at each other. It seemed like maybe matchmaking was in the air today.

Still, someone had been chucked into a privy, and we needed to focus on the matter at hand. As Mika dug through the last of the debris and then spent a few minutes sifting through the dirt at the bottom of the pit, Summer assembled the skeleton and said, "I can't be sure, but it looks like a man's body. I think this is a man's pelvis."

I sighed. The more we learned about this person, I knew from experience, the more the sadness of the situation would sink in. Once a pile of bones got the characteristics of a human being, things got a whole lot more real.

"Anything else strike you?" Santiago asked.

"You mean besides this giant slice through one rib? No not much," Summer said as she stood up.

"Seems pretty certain you found the murder weapon, Mika," Santiago said, and then he took out his phone and called the coroner.

DEPUTY WINSLOW ARRIVED a few minutes later with assurances that everything was secure at Saul's lot. "He'll lock up tight tonight, and as long as we can keep this quiet until we can review the evidence tomorrow, we shouldn't have to worry about people snooping around."

Santiago looked at each of us in turn. "That means you can't say a word to anyone, not even your dad or Lucille, Pais," he said as he held my gaze.

"I understand," I said, and I did. But it was always so hard for me not to talk about things. I had to make a firm commitment to myself that I wouldn't say anything. Fortunately, Sawyer was staying the night with them and then going to his dad's in the morning, so hopefully I wouldn't have to see any of them until the news was already out.

Just then, an old, red Chevy pickup drove by very slowly, and because it was only poking along, we all turned to stare at it. It was only when it was past us that we realized the driver – as well as any other driver who had come by in the last half hour – may have been able to see the bones laid out beside the privy hole. It was going to be hard to keep this quiet.

"I'm going to issue a statement, if it's okay with you, Sheriff, that we found the remains of a cow out in the old barn in Lucky Hollow. Say it looked like it had fallen into an old privy and broken a leg and ask the farmers around to let us know who might have lost a cow a couple decades back."

Santiago smiled. "Good plan. Throw people off and maybe get some folks giving us info we need. I like it Savannah." Santiago clapped her on the back and grinned.

"We'll have to play that up tonight at dinner, too. Talk about the poor animal and stuff, really sell it," I said.

"I am a really good actor," Chris said as Dom groaned.

"No monologues at dinner," Dom said. "You have to promise."

"Is this a thing?" Mika asked Chris.

"I like to memorize beautiful language," Chris said before he winked at Mika, "You never know when you might meet a woman who deserves to be serenaded with words."

I laughed a bit too loudly and then quickly turned to the police officers and said, "Now what?"

"Now we wait, and I practice due diligence and get in the

hole." He glanced at Mika. "I'm sure you found all the remains, but I need to do my job."

"Of course," Mika said. "I would feel horrible if some part of this poor person was still down there."

While Santiago lowered himself into the hole, we all watched as that same pickup drove by again, and this time, Summer said, "I think that's one of the guys who came by my place last week."

"You think their visit has something to do with this," Savannah asked.

Summer shrugged. "I'm not sure." Then she told everyone else about the two men who had come by her house a few days earlier. "They were definitely warning me off, but I didn't make much of it until today."

"Did they tell you their names?" Savannah asked.

"Homer Salis and Lee Sutton," she said.

I gasped. "My dad came to see you?"

3

The coroner's van arrived shortly after, which was good because when Santiago told me I needed to stop talking to Summer about my dad's visit to her house, I found it very hard to do anything else. The distraction of watching the coroner examine the bones and then carefully load them into her van gave me something else to focus on. For the moment.

But as soon as Savannah and Santiago loaded up the crates of bottles and Savannah headed back into town to catalog them, I couldn't help myself. "My dad warned you not to disturb this barn?" I asked again.

"I didn't know he was your dad, Paisley," she said. "Maybe I should have thought of that because of the last name, but a lot of folks around here share a name and aren't close kin. Just look at the Shiffletts." She blushed as she looked over at Santiago, Sheriff Shifflett. "Sorry."

"No need to apologize. It's true, and you couldn't have known that Lee was Paisley's father, but now, we need to stop talking about this until I can get your statement," Santiago said. "Have time to give it now?"

"Sure," Summer said, "if you do."

"Pais, could you and Mika head into town to get us a table at the Inn? Guys, you can give Summer and me a ride, right?" Santiago asked.

"Sure thing. We'll wait in the car," Dom said, and the two men walked Mika and me over to my Subaru. "Actually, Paisley, mind if I ride with you? I wanted to ask you some more about your business." He winked at me. "Mika, would you mind keeping Chris company?"

I rolled my eyes as I thought my friend would never fall for such an obvious ploy, but she said, "Sure. Sounds like fun. See you in a few, Pais," and got right into the front seat of Chris's huge pickup, I smiled. "I think she's smitten," I said to Dom as I climbed into my driver's seat.

"I *know* he is," Dom said. "I haven't seen him smile that much in years except when Jill is around." He drummed his hand against the dashboard. "She'll be kind to him, right?"

"Are you kidding? Mika is the kindest person I know, to a fault sometimes. He won't take advantage of that, will he?"

Dom shook his head. "Chris is a straight-up good guy. He's had a hard run of it since his wife died a few years ago. Single dad. Lost his job as a chef. It was rough for a bit, but when he took what he loved – cooking with his daughter – and made it into a business, everything started to turn around."

I smiled and thought back over the last couple years of my life – my split with Sawyer's dad, the need to build my own business to support the two of us, a new house to care for – and I almost laughed out loud for joy. All my hard work, all the things I had dreamed and imagined, all of them had come to life. Even a sweet, kind, self-sufficient man who didn't need me but wanted me. All of it was there, and I could absolutely understand how Chris might feel in this moment when things got so much better. I was excited for him . . . and excited for how Mika might be a part of that for him and he for her. "Good.

That all sounds good," I said. I didn't know Dom very well, and I didn't think it quite appropriate to put my over-hoping joy at Mika and Chris's connection on him. At least not yet.

We rode in silence for a few minutes, and then he said, "I actually wasn't totally BS-ing back there when I said I had questions about your business. I have this client, and she's interested in starting a thrift store of sorts, all mid-century modern stuff, but she doesn't know much about running a business. Any tips you'd give her?"

I smiled. "Lots. Give her my number, and we can meet up and talk. I might even be able to work with her to get merchandise."

"Really? That's very nice of you. I don't want to impose, and I know she wouldn't either," Dom said.

I glanced over at him as I turned onto Main Street and parked up from the Inn by Mika's shop. "It's not an imposition. I really believe in helping other women build their businesses. I'd be happy to help, especially since what she and I do are similar. I bet Summer would help, too. She's decorated her entire house from things she picked up in thrift stores."

"Nice. I'll ask her." He blushed a little around his collar and then stepped out of the car. Mika and Chris pulled up just behind us, and when they walked over, they were both laughing. "You have to get Chris to tell you the story of the first time he made mac and cheese for Jill, Pais." She put her hand on Chris's arm. "You'll pee your pants."

"Well, when you put it that way," I said, "why wouldn't I want to hear it?" I rolled my eyes and led the way toward the Inn.

Mika said that Santi had sent them on and Summer was bringing him and joining them for dinner. We were on the early side for a weekend dinner, so it wasn't hard for the host to find a table for six in a quiet corner. While we waited for Santiago and Summer to join us, we ordered drinks – beer for most of us and a dirty martini for me. Then we went ahead and got some stuffed mushrooms and an order of nachos as starters. It was going to be a long weekend, and it felt like we could probably all use a little extra something tonight. I knew Santiago wouldn't mind, and I made a point to save some of both appetizers.

When he and Summer came in about a half-hour later, Dom pulled out the chair next to him for Summer while I patted the one next to me for the sheriff. He kissed my cheek and looked at the small plate in front of him. "Thanks for saving some for me." He looked at his friends. "How steep is my bill already?"

"This is my fifth beer, buddy, so get your AmEx ready?" Chris joked as he nursed his first beer.

"I had four other appetizers, but the server already took the plates," Dom added. "You're lucky Paisley guarded that sample with her life or you'd be missing out on the best mushrooms in the state."

"I had to throw my body in front of them to stave off Dom's fork, I'll have you know," I said. "You're worth it, though."

He grinned at me as he stuffed the last of his mushrooms into his mouth and then kissed me on the lips. "Thank you," he mumbled against my mouth.

"You're welcome," I said with a laugh. Then, as silence descended, I made a suggestion. "Maybe tonight, we don't talk about what – I mean, who – we found today. Would that be okay with everyone?"

Santiago squeezed my knee under the table as he nodded. "I like that plan. Any objections?"

"I move we accept Paisley's motion," Summer said.

"Second," Dom added. "All in favor?"

A resounding "aye" rose up from the table, and our server must have decided it was time to get more food into us because she hustled over and took our orders.

The rest of the evening was relaxing and fun. We chatted about our jobs, about our families, and about our town. In fact, the most riled up we got was when we started talking about the highspeed internet that kept being promised by our board of supervisors but still hadn't come in. "I tried to load a Power-Point presentation the other day," Santiago said, "and it said it would take *forty-nine hours* to load."

I groaned. For me as a small business owner, the internet was a source of daily frustration, for Mika, too, so we spent some time strategizing how we could put pressure on the board to get things moving.

But beyond that, we mostly laughed and drank a couple too many beers and then allowed our designated drivers to get us home or walk us home in the case of Chris and Mika. There was definitely something burgeoning there, and I was here for it.

Fortunately, my DD was the sheriff, and after he dropped Dom and Summer off, he came back to my house, where we switched to hot tea and settled into the cooling evening on the porch.

Santiago was still very professional about how we discussed his cases, and he never revealed anything, even to me, that would put his investigations or someone else's privacy in danger. But we had come to a place in our relationship where I was, as he said, his sounding board when he needed to figure something out.

Tonight, he needed to do a lot of figuring, so I sipped my tea and listened.

"That body had been there a long time. Decades, right? I mean you said some of those bottles were from the late 1800s."

I nodded and sipped. I'd learned over the past few months that he knew most of the answers to his own questions, and it was best if I simply gave him someone to share his thoughts with.

"The question, I guess, is whether the body was above those bottles or below them. I suppose we should have been keeping things in the order in which they came out of the hole, but how could we know we needed to do that?" His face had taken on the distant gaze I recognized as his "thinking face."

As he stared out across the wildflower meadow below my house, I studied his face. He was handsome in a quiet way: Strong jaw, wonderful black hair, a soft mouth. But his face wasn't one that would be on magazine pages; instead, it was the face of someone you trusted, which of course was perfect in his role as sheriff, especially in a community that distrusted authority for a variety of reasons. He had fought hard to get where he was, and he kept fighting to keep not only his position as an elected officer but to actually serve the community he loved. That's one of the things I loved about him.

I cleared my throat as I realized that my thoughts had turned to love, something I wasn't quite ready to confess yet, but fortunately, Santiago didn't seem to notice because he turned to me and said, "Is there a way to date glass?"

"Sure," I said. "I don't know the specifics, but I know the way it was made matters and so does the top. I can get some resources together and come over tomorrow and help you sort them by date if that would help."

He nodded. "I think it would. I know that we don't know exactly where in the pit we were when Mika found the man's skull, but I think having some sense of how old things are might help us find out how he ended up there."

"Makes sense," I said. "Is it possible that someone just tried to bury a person who died naturally there?" Even as I said the words, I realized how ridiculous that sounded, especially if the body was from a time when people buried their loved ones, often in their own backyards.

Santiago grinned. "Not likely, Pais, but I appreciate that you are not thinking the worst about whoever did this. That's a fresh perspective." He sighed. "Sadly, though, I think we're probably looking at a death that someone wanted to keep hidden, and well hidden, too."

I dropped my head. "I figured that was the case, but you know me, always hopeful." I looked up and smiled at my boyfriend.

"That's one of the reasons I lo--, I like you so much," Santiago said as a blush came to his cheeks. "You are amazing," he whispered as he leaned over and kissed me.

I tried to slow my heart rate as I thought about the word he almost said, but the tenderness of his kiss made that completely impossible.

THE NEXT DAY I woke to one of those early fall mornings that steal my breath every year. It was only fifty degrees, and the warmth of the sun was lifting steam off the roof of the chicken coop when I went out to see the girls. Their eggs were wonderfully warm against my hand, and I went right back in and cooked up a great omelette for myself before heading into town for my usual Saturday work day at Mika's shop. It was early, so she wasn't even open yet. But I knew my friend, and sure enough, the door was unlocked and the coffee was brewed.

She was knitting and listening to music in one of the chairs in the cozy nook, and when she heard the door open, she smiled and slid the insulated carafe of coffee across the table toward my seat. I had lots of work to do, and I had told Santiago I'd be over at ten to look at the bottles with him. But I made the executive decision as the CEO of my business to spend this hour sewing with my friend. I took out my latest cross-stitch project and began to stitch.

I had decided to get ambitious since my last project had been mostly a one-colored tractor for Sawyer's room. This time, I was taking on a project by my favorite designer, Teresa Wentzler. It was her Father Winter pattern, and it included a ton of tiny stitches and blended threads, so the piece was a challenge. But I loved the idea of having it – with the name of our farm-house, Sanctuary, stitched into the bottom panel so I could hang it by the fireplace this winter. Or next winter. Probably next winter at this rate.

I picked up a bobbin of light pink thread and found the corresponding lavender color to blend as Mika whizzed through another row of the shawl she was knitting to sell. It was a gorgeous hunter green, and I decided that if my first week of business at the shop hit my goals, I was going to buy it for myself. It was lovely. Of course, I'd have to keep my purchase secret, send in a decoy to buy it or Mika would try to just give it to me.

"So what's on your work agenda for today?" Mika asked, as she did every week.

I always appreciated the question because it forced me to plan ahead, not just get caught up in whatever task appeared at the moment. "I need to get the newsletter done and do some social media posts about the shop opening next weekend." I sighed. "I'm going to miss my Saturdays here with you."

Mika grinned. "Actually, I've been meaning to talk to you about that. I wondered if I could come work at your store next weekend. Mrs. Stephenson said she'd cover here, and I'd love to help out on your first day."

Tears sprung to my eyes. "I would love that. Thank you."

"Yay, and maybe if I sit and knit, it'll help sell some of my things, too. Speaking of which, can I show you the pieces I thought we could display there?" she asked as she stood up and pulled a tote out from behind her chair.

"Definitely." I finished the row I was stitching and then sat forward. "Let me see."

Mika held up a beautiful pair of chunky mittens in a lovely gray wool. "I have a few pairs of these in different colors. And I have this." It was a stunning cable-knit sweater in a blue-green that made me think of the ocean in winter.

"Wow, those are amazing. I think they'll sell quickly. What else?"

She showed me a couple of baby blankets and two children's sweaters that were beyond adorable. But it was her last set of items that most piqued my interest. "These are cowls. You wear them like scarves, but they just button up."

Each of them was thick and full, and I could just imagine putting one on under my winter coat and feeling so cozy. The colors she had chosen were gorgeous too – bright purples and blues, a hot pink that someone fun would adore, and a very lovely brown that tended toward rust. "I love these, Mika. If you can make more, I think they'll do really well. Maybe Dad can make a rack to display them?"

"Ooh, do you think he would?" she asked.

I rolled my eyes. "For you, he'd build an entire display set. Want me to ask him?"

"Yes please," she said as she tucked her creations back in their bin. "I'll bring these over later in the week to set up?"

"Sounds good," I said as I took out my phone to text Dad. I sent the message and then packed up my own sewing. "I need to get over to the sheriff's office for a bit." I told Mika about how we were going to try to date the bottles. "Be back with lunch in a couple of hours?"

"Good luck, and yes, please. My treat," she said.

"Absolutely not," I said firmly. Mika's business was picking up, especially with her new stall at the city market, but now that she was going to be selling at my shop, too, she'd had to hire a young woman to staff the market stall, and she was working every spare minute to make items to sell as well as running her own business. She was well on her way to having a really good income, but she wasn't there yet, not with the outlay for all the yarn and staffing.

As I walked up the street to the sheriff's office, I thought about how far I had come in just the last year. I had more offers to salvage than I could take on, many at no cost to me beyond the crew and gasoline from Saul, who kept cutting me a break on even those expenses despite my protests. My online auctions were still doing well, and I was launching my own online store in conjunction with the brick-and-mortar one next week. I had never in my life had so much cash and found so much joy in anything I'd done, and the least I could do was share it with my best friend.

When I walked in the front door of the station, the dispatcher waved me right back to the conference room, where I found Santiago and Savannah in front of the table spread with our bottles. They were still divided by color, and while the look was visually very pleasing, what with the rainbow of browns to blues to greens to clears, color wasn't going to be especially helpful here.

Instead, I texted both of them a link to a great website I'd found by a man named Reggie Lynch, who was a bottle expert, and the three of us set about looking at seams and toppers, studying the patent marks on the bottom. Before long, we had a clear sense that most of the bottles were from around 1940 to 1960. A few were earlier, but nothing was as old as I had thought it would be. Nothing from earlier than 1920, certainly. That was a bit disappointing for me in terms of sales, but from the perspective of solving a mystery, a more focused and more recent date was definitely good.

"So it looks like the person was put into the pit sometime in the 40s or 50s," Savannah said. She picked up a green glass piece that was seamless from top to bottom, consulted the pattern mark, and added it to the large collection of glass from the 1940s.

"Does indeed," Santiago said. He turned to me. "Unless you

see a bottle that really catches your eye, Pais, I think we've got enough information to go on."

I scanned the table a last time but then shook my head. "As far as I can see, it's more of the same. But if you want, I have another half hour or so, and I can sort the rest, or at least more of them."

Santiago smiled but shook his head. "That's really not necessary, but I appreciate the offer." He took a photo of the bottles as they were sorted on the table. "In fact, since a tech checked them for evidence last night, you can take them with you if you want. We didn't find anything telling, and I know they'd make a good addition to your opening next week."

Savannah snapped her fingers. "That's right. Your new store. Need help setting up?"

"Definitely," I said, "whenever you're free. I'll have food, and we'll knock out the last of the arrangements."

"I'll get one of the guys to cover for you if you want. That way, we can both be there," Santiago added.

The police force in Octonia was tiny, just Santiago and Savannah really, but recently, Santiago had brought on two new part-time deputies, young men who were from the county and who really loved the people here. It was good for everyone, especially the two full-time officers, since it gave them a few more evenings and weekends free.

"That would be great," Savannah said. "I'll bring some special lemonade." She made air quotes around the word *special*, and I laughed.

"Great. Alright, Sheriff Shifflett, can I ask your help in loading up these bottles? I'm parked down by Mika's. Want me to bring the car around?" I asked.

"Nope. I could use the exercise." He filled two of the crates and then lifted one in each arm while I hefted the final remaining crate into both of my arms. "You ready?"

I grinned. "Yes, sir. Can I get the gun show after?"

Savannah cackled, and Santiago rolled his eyes as we headed out to the street and up to my car. I opened the hatch with my keyring, and Santiago carefully arranged the crates with my cat Beauregard's blanket between them to prevent them from sliding. Beau would not be happy that he did not give his permission, but since he was rarely happy anyway, I didn't care.

After I shut the hatch, Santiago leaned against the car and said, "So have you talked to your dad?"

I sighed and shook my head. I'd thought about calling him this morning to see why he'd visited Summer, but I didn't want to sound like I was accusing him of something."

"Are you accusing him of something?"

I fluttered my lips. "Maybe? I mean why would he warn Summer away from changing the barn but not tell me the same thing. Why would he care at all?"

"It's a good question," Santiago said. "Your call – but one of us has to talk to him. If you'd prefer I do it, I can, but we might get a more truthful answer if you bring it up casually."

"Right," I said as I bit off a fingernail I'd been growing out for over a week, a major feat for me. "But I'm not a police officer, so anything he tells me is hearsay, right?"

"I'm going to send you to law school so that you get real knowledge instead of TV police knowledge," he said with a laugh. "Technically, yes, but if it's a simple explanation – lead-based paint, worry about destroying a landmark – something like that, then there's nothing that's a big deal there."

I shuddered. "And if it is a big deal . . . or if he won't tell me . . ."

"Then, I'll have to bring him in." Santiago sighed and pulled me against his side. "Either way, maybe it's best to give him a chance to explain without getting me involved."

"Yeah. That makes sense." I dropped my head onto his shoulder. "And if it's not good, I guess it doesn't really matter who hears it first." I groaned and pulled my phone out of my pocket. "Here goes," I said as I pressed my dad's photo in my contacts.

"I'll wait inside. Give you some privacy." He walked into Mika's store, and I waited for dad to pick up the phone. Or rather, I both hoped he wouldn't and that he would. Part of me didn't want to do this at all, and part of me just wanted to get it over with.

Just when I figured Dad had done his usual and left his phone somewhere that he couldn't hear it, my step-mom Lucille picked up. "Hi Pais, your dad is in the garden. What's up?"

My dad and step-mom shared everything, so I knew that whatever I told him he was going to tell her anyway. I said, "I need to talk to Dad about the octagonal barn I took down yesterday."

Lucille sighed. "I told him not to get involved, to just let things evolve as they would. What happened?"

"We found a body," I said.

"Where are you? We're coming over," she said.

4

I told Santiago they were on their way to Mika's, and he
decided to go back to work, give us some space to talk this
through.

As soon as Dad walked into Mika's shop, I knew this was going
to be a hard conversation. His face was drawn, and his shoulders
slumped so far forward that he looked like he was beginning to
bend over and pick up something off the floor. I was glad Mika and
Lucille were there because when my dad looked like this, he could
get petulant and quiet. I needed people to help me bring him out.

Fortunately, Lucille was a no-nonsense woman, and she
spoke straight and true when she needed to. So as soon as we
sat down, she said, "Lee, tell Paisley what you know about that
barn." Then she looked at me, "I haven't told him what you told
me yet, Pais. Figured it was better to let this all come out to the
fore without any prep."

I nodded. "Please, Dad. I know you went to see Summer
Ross. Why?"

Dad stared at the floor in front of where his forearms sat on
his knees, and for a minute, I thought he was going to with-

draw, not answer, just sit there staring and acting like he hadn't heard my question. But then, Lucille put a hand on his leg. He looked over at her, and then met my gaze.

"I was scared, Paisley. Scared you'd find what I expect it is you found." He let out a slow stream of breath. "You found him, didn't you?"

"Start from the beginning, Daddy," I said. I'd learned enough from Santiago to understand it was better, even with my dad, to not reveal anything that I didn't need to share just yet. As a daughter, I wanted to make my dad feel better, but right now, I needed to focus on what was most important, figuring out what happened to the man in the privy pit. "Please."

Dad took a long, slow breath. "It was 1945 Your grandfather was over in Germany in the Army. He told me the story, even though he wasn't here." Dad met my gaze. "He just knew the story, Pais. He was across the ocean when it happened."

"Got it," I said.

"Apparently, folks here were pretty heated up about the attack on Pearl Harbor. Lots of the young men enlisted even before the draft called them up. Your granddaddy was one of those men. He was proud to serve." I knew that was true, but I also knew that war had messed up my grandfather. He never would talk about it much, except to tell jokes, and after he died, I found more notes and images from his time there. It had been brutal, for everyone.

Dad continued. "Some of the men, though, they didn't want to fight. For most of those guys, it was just about wanting and needing to be home to take care of their families. Of course, they weren't given a choice in the matter and got drafted anyway."

I nodded. "Okay." I was waiting for how all this tied into the body we'd found in the pit, but I knew better than to push my daddy to talk faster than he wanted. He'd just get agitated and clam up.

"Daddy said a couple of guys went to extremes to stay home, though. The religious ones registered as conscientious objectors, and lots of those men worked for the CPS, even had a camp up here in the mountains," Dad said.

"CPS?" Mika asked.

"Civilian Public Service. They did things like build roads and plant trees to stop erosion. That kind of thing." He sighed. "But some guys just tried to avoid all kinds of service. One fellow made it to Canada, I heard, but a couple others laid low around here and hid when people came looking for them."

I felt a pit growing in my stomach as this story unfolded, but I stayed quiet.

"One of these men was a guy named Leo Farrow. Everyone called him Sheepy, though. He just out and out refused to serve in any capacity. Wouldn't run either, and while he didn't make a show of himself, he wasn't too shy about being out in public either. Went to church on Sundays. Showed up for the county fair. That kind of thing." Dad shook his head.

"According to your grandaddy, folks finally had enough of protecting Sheepy while the men they loved died in a terrible war. So one night, a few of the men left in town here went over, picked him up, and took care of the problem." Dad scrubbed a hand over his face. "Rumor had it they dumped him out at the barn in the hollow there."

"Do you know who did it, Daddy?"

Dad sat back, crossed his arms, and looked at me. "That's all I have to say about that to you, Paisley girl."

I stared at him for a minute and when I got over my shock, I said, "Dad, are the men who did this still alive? Are you protecting them?"

"It was a long time ago, Paisley. Leave it be." He held my

eyes, and when I didn't look away, his jaw tightened, and he finally flashed his eyes to the floor.

"Daddy, a man was killed, and Mika found his skull in a toilet pit." I took a breath. "I'm not out to get someone here. But this man, Leo Farrow, deserves justice, don't you think?"

Dad stood up and headed toward the door. "I'm taking a walk," he said with a quick glance at Lucille, and then he was gone.

"What in the world?!" Mika said as the door swung shut behind my father.

Lucille shook her head. "I have no idea. Something's going on." She stood and followed him out the door.

"Do you think Santiago will want to talk to him now?" Mika asked, her train of thought about three steps ahead of mine. I was still staring at the door.

I tugged my eyes over to meet those of my best friend and sighed. "I need to call him. Is it okay with you if he comes here? Somehow, having this conversation at the police station feels too hard just now."

"Of course," she said. "Why don't you just text him while you watch the shop, and I'll go get us some lunch?"

"That would be nice. Thanks." I moved over behind the register and took out my phone again. "Talked to Dad. At Mika's. Can you come?" I typed.

"Be there in five." His answer was almost immediate, and I felt a little of the lump that had gathered in my throat break up. At least I wasn't in this alone.

Before I tucked my phone back in my pocket, I shot Lucille a note to tell her Santiago was on his way, just in case she and Dad headed back. I didn't want my father to feel blindsided.

She wrote back. "We're way out of town and still walking. It'll be a while before he's ready to come back."

I sighed and let tears finally fall. I couldn't believe my dad. I knew that while Santiago would do all he could, the more my father avoided this situation, the worse it would be for him.

"Don't worry, Paisley," Lucille's second message said. "He will come back."

I sent a thumbs up and then stowed my phone beneath the register. I didn't want to be checking it for messages every ten seconds.

Mika and Santiago came in the door together, and while I didn't feel hungry at the moment, I was glad to see she'd brought me a Dr. Pepper with my grilled cheese and mushroom sandwich. Sometimes, nothing helped like a jolt of sugar and a blast of caffeine. I took a long pull from the straw as Santiago and I settled into the cozy corner and Mika moved to the front of the store to straighten shelves, greet customers, and give us some privacy.

"I take it you don't have good news," Santiago said as he pulled his chair closer to mine.

I shook my head. "He won't tell me who killed him."

Santiago sat back. "He knows?"

I took a deep breath. "I think so." Then, I told Santiago all that Dad had said about Leo Farrow and avoiding the draft and the vigilante justice that Dad said had taken place. "There's a piece he's not telling me, though, Santi."

"And you think that piece identifies the killers?" he asked.

I nodded and then sighed. "My dad is usually so reasonable, so aware that the past, no matter how far distant, isn't really that far away. But he's acting like his best friend—" I stopped talking abruptly and looked down away from Santiago's gaze.

"Homer," Santiago said quietly.

As soon as I had thought of Dad's best friend, the man who had gone to see Summer Ross with him, I knew. Homer Salis was mixed up in this somehow. I nodded and looked back up at Santi. "I think so."

For a few moments, we sat in silence, and the possibilities of what this could mean spooled through my mind until the bell rang over the door and Dad and Lucille came in. I stood up, hugged my dad, and then made a silent decision to let Santiago handle this moment.

"Lee," Santiago said as he extended a hand to my dad. "Good to see you. Am I right in understanding that you might know something I should know about the person we found at the old barn?"

Dad looked at his wife and then at me before he said, "I do." He looked up at the ceiling and then said, "It was Homer's father."

My stomach dropped into my ankles, but I managed to hold back my gasp. It wasn't going to make it any easier for my dad if he had to deal with my response as well as his own complex emotions at this moment.

"I see," Santiago said. "So Homer told you this?"

Dad shook his head. "Not exactly." He stared at the floor. "I was there."

This time, even my best attempts at underreacting were overwhelmed by shock, and I said, "What?!"

"I was only four, but I was there." Dad stared at the floor as he spoke. "I didn't really know what was happening then. Neither did Homer. But I saw Mr. Salis drop something wrapped in a rug down in that hole. I didn't know then, but when I was older, I figured it out."

"And you didn't come forward because it was your friend's dad?" Santiago asked.

Dad shook his head. "No. By the time I figured it out, Mr. Salis was dead. Cancer." He looked up at me. "So I figured what was the point but to make Homer's life harder." He shook his head slightly. "I didn't want to do that. Not after he watched his dad die like he did."

I didn't know the whole story of Homer's dad, but I knew

that he hadn't been a kind man, abusive probably, and that his death had been long and slow. And while some people softened when they became ill, according to Dad, Homer's father became as hard as flint and mean as a cornered copperhead. He had died when Homer and Dad were seventeen, so just when Homer could have used a father to guide him, he'd gotten sick, gotten meaner, and then died at home with his wife and Homer. The whole story sounded like something from a gothic short story.

Santiago nodded. "You were how old when he died?"

"Just a teenager." His eyes were sorrowful as he met Santiago's gaze. "I thought I was doing the right thing."

I understood my dad's decision back then, even if I didn't agree with it, but a few minutes ago, what had that been about? A man had been killed, and even if his murderer was long dead, the man still deserved justice. Dad looked so sad, though, that I decided to just table that question for now.

"So Mr. Salis – what was his first name?" Santiago asked.

"James, Jimmy," Dad answered.

Santiago made a note. "Jimmy Salis was the only man there then." He didn't ask. He made a statement, or at least it sounded like a statement, but I knew Santi well enough by now to know his tactics. Sometimes his statements were really open doors so people could volunteer information without feeling like they were forced.

"I didn't say that," Dad mumbled.

Without looking up, Santiago said, "I see. Who else was there?" His voice was quiet but forceful.

For a minute, I thought Dad wasn't going to answer. But then he said, "I guess you need to know. Stephen Davis, Melvin Smith, and Ace Watkins." Dad was sitting up now, his decision made and his choice clear.

"To your knowledge, were all these men involved in the

death of Leo Farrow?" Santiago asked, the façade of casualness gone.

Dad shook his head. "I honestly don't know. I just know that those four men were there when Farrow's body got dumped." Dad met my gaze. "To be clear, I can't even say for sure it was Farrow's body in that rug. I never saw it. But it seems likely."

Santiago nodded. "It does. But that is good information to know. So how do you know the other men were involved?"

"Mr. Salis talked about it, said that the four of them had taken care of a problem." Dad shook his head. "He was so proud."

I groaned. The human ability to be confident in wrong-doing never failed to astound me.

"Understood," Santiago said as he stood. "Now, as two of these men are still alive, I need all of you to give me your word you will not say anything about what we've discussed to anyone. I need to investigate, and I need to do that without interference. Am I clear?"

If we hadn't understood just by the nature of what he requested, we would have by the tone of his voice. Santiago was angry, and while he was our friend, I also knew that if we crossed him, he wouldn't hesitate to do his job. All of us nodded.

"I will need to talk to Homer, Lee," he said to my dad as he handed dad his business card. "It would be better if he called me. But if he doesn't reach out by the end of the day, I will be going to see him tonight. I'm sure you understand."

Dad nodded and tucked the card in his breast pocket before he reached out to help Lucille up. "We'll go see him now," he said, and the two of them walked toward the door as Lucille turned back toward me and made a "phone me" sign.

I nodded and then gave my boyfriend a hug before he headed out the door. I wanted to say something, to assure him, to cheer him on, but I knew none of that was appropriate. We were talking about a murder here, a murder my dad had kept secret , and nothing I was going to say could help. Not a thing.

He looked at me, shrugged, and walked out.

I DECIDED to spend the better part of the next two hours creating a rainbow display of worsted weight yarn for Mika. I needed to do something simple that didn't require me to think too hard about anything because my mind was spinning. I had so much to do for my business and for the opening in a few days, but I knew myself. If I didn't give myself time to process, I'd never get anything meaningful done.

Fortunately, Mika had Mrs. Stephenson to run the shop for the afternoon, and so she and I sat in a back corner with crates and stacks of yarn while I spun out all the random thoughts that were twirling in my head.

I talked through my frustration with my dad a bit and then through the sadness I felt about him having witnessed something so horrible as a child. Then I speculated how hard this must be for Homer and for my Dad in turn, and how conflicted they must feel about turning in their elders for a nearly eighty-year-old crime. Then, I wondered how Lucille was doing with all this, and finally my thoughts settled into concerns about Santiago and how he must have to traverse hurdles like this as a police officer in our small town.

After I had rambled through my anxieties about the people I loved for a good forty-five minutes, Mika finally put a hand on my arm and said, "But Paisley, how do you feel about all this?"

I looked at her and said, "I just told you how I feel. Weren't you listening?" I could hear the huff in my voice, but I was too tired to care.

"No, Pais, what you told me was how you felt about how everyone else may or may not be feeling. You didn't tell me how you feel. Are you mad at your dad for keeping this secret?

Relieved he came forward now? Worried about him and Santiago? Concerned this might affect your relationship with your boyfriend?"

I stared at her for a long moment, and then I started to cry. "Yes, I'm worried about all those things. So worried." I let the tears fall for a few moments before I whispered, "This is terrifying."

Mika removed the stack of purple from my hands, careful to not disturb the beautiful ombre I had made, and then hugged me. "I'm sure it is, Pais. Of course it is. But Santiago is a good man, and so is your dad. It will all be okay."

"Are you sure?" I asked in a voice that sounded even pitiful to me.

"I'm sure," she said and then cradled my head against her shoulder for a few more minutes. Then, she squeezed my head, pushed me gently away, and said, "Let's get this rainbow up because you have a store to open."

When I looked up, my friend was standing over me with her hand extended and a soft smile on her face. She looked so kind with her freckled nose and gentle wrinkles at the corner of her eyes. I didn't know how I'd gotten so lucky to have a friend like her.

Which is why I knew exactly what she'd say when I stood, grabbed the array of purple yarn and said, "So, Chris?"

"He's nice," she said and turned away from me.

"I knew you liked him," I said. "Nice" had always been Mika's word for someone attractive. "Are you going to see him?"

As she picked up the pieces of plastic we'd discarded around the floor, Mika said, "Oh, probably sometime."

I took her by the shoulders and forced her to face me. "And by sometime you mean specifically when?"

"Tonight at dinner." A blush ran from her collar to her hairline, and she was grinning.

"And you weren't going to tell me?" I rolled my eyes. "Some friend."

"We had a little something going on," Mika said as she lightly punched my shoulder. "Want to join us?"

"No way. First dates are not fun for anyone but the dating pair." I'd double dated with friends on a few firsts when I was younger, and my date and I always ended up cringing while they got their footing and asked awkward questions. It was better to not have an audience for those first few moments, especially if they didn't go well.

Not that I thought Mika's date with Chris wouldn't go well. I expected it to go swimmingly, but I didn't need to witness them get to swimming. Nope. "You guys have fun, and let me know when I need to send the possible 'rescue' text to get you out."

"Nine? We're meeting at seven, so two hours should give me enough time to know. If I don't answer, don't worry," she said as the color deepened on her cheeks.

"Got it. But my no-worry zone only extends until eleven. If I don't hear from you by then, I will turn the worry knob up to ten." I stared at her. "Text by eleven with an all clear if things are going well, okay?"

"Absolutely. Besides, if I'm up at eleven still, I'll need your help to get home. I haven't stayed up past ten in a decade." She laughed.

"Well, maybe now you'll have a reason." I chuckled and headed toward the Cozy Covey to get to work. I was still worried about my dad and about Santiago too, but it was fun to think about Mika's date and with that and the shop opening, I had plenty to distract me for a while.

TWO HOURS, a newsletter, and a press release later, I was still deep in my work, now checking my online inventory system and adding in the items Mika had made for sale. Things were starting to feel ready for next weekend, but I knew I had a lot more to do. I decided I could put off the computer work for the rest of the day and told Mika I was heading over to the shop to display her things and get some stuff in order.

"You need my help?" she asked as she watched Mrs. Stephenson talk with a teenage girl who was beginning her first knitting project. Just then, a group of women from a nearby church came in, and Mika's attention spun to them before coming back to me.

"Nope. The quiet space on my own will give me time to experiment." I winked at her. "Text you at nine."

The drive to the shop was short, but I rolled the windows down and enjoyed the fresh air as I looked to see if I could see a hint of autumn color on the dogwoods yet. They were always my first sign that autumn was well on the way.

At the shop, Saul's crew was hard at work arranging a new shipment of lumber in their tall pole barn and loading up their dump truck with sand, and I was grateful for their presence and the background noise of the forklifts and front-end loaders. I did feel a pang of absence since Sawyer wasn't here to see the "big equipment" running, but I knew he was having fun camping with his dad and let the guilt over something I couldn't control go.

Instead, I threw myself into rearranging all the items in the shop. I had the bottles to work in now as well as Mika's items. So I took everything down, dusted the shelves so that they would be as clean as they possibly could in the midst of a construction zone, and began replacing items in the back corner, where I had decided I would make a rainbow of sorts with the bottles we'd found.

I didn't have the reds or oranges, but I substituted in brown then added the green and blue. Finally, I did an array of transparent glass at the end. Not exactly ROY G BIV but still pretty and easy to maintain. That was key in a business like this. I couldn't be working all the time to arrange the shelves when I needed to be greeting customers and bringing in new inventory, too.

Mika's items were next, and I had just set one pair of fluffy wool mittens next to an intricate Victorian corbel when the door of my shed banged open hard enough to shake the glass in the door. I spun around to see an older white man with a gaunt face and thin white hair staring at me. In his hand, he held a rusty hook.

5

I recognized the man almost instantly, but it took me a second to place him. And when I did, my heart began to dance. It was Ace Watkins. I'd known him all my life as the oldest man in town at what had to now be almost a hundred. He was famous for handing out sticks of Juicy Fruit gum to the children around town, and if he hadn't been so charming and so gentle, he probably would have scared a lot of parents in this age where it seemed we were expected to guard our children from even the most innocent of potentially dangerous experiences.

But today, he didn't look like his genial, kind self. Today, he looked outright mad, and I thought I knew why. Word must have reached him about the body in the privy, and now he was here to stop me from running my mouth.

I was cornered, and while my phone was nearby on the counter where the register would soon stand, I didn't want to make any sudden movements in case that hook was something Ace was ready to use. So I took a deep breath, smiled brightly, and said, "Mr. Watkins, it's so good to see you. Can I help you with something?"

As if he had flipped a switch, Ace's look of menace turned into a wide grin, and he said, "Actually, I'm hoping I can help you. First, let me say how sorry I am that you had to find that poor boy's body yesterday."

I had to work hard to keep my mouth from falling open, but I stayed quiet and tried to look sanguine, not shocked. "Thank you. It was a horrible thing."

"So horrible. Your daddy and I were just talking about it. I'm afraid he had some faulty memories about that day, but I think he's clear now." He smiled at me and nodded, and I felt a small chill tickle up my spine. "But anyway, that's not why I'm here."

I nodded again and said, "Okay. What can I do for you?"

He held the hook up toward me. "I have a bunch of these old farm implements that I haven't gotten around to scrapping yet, and your daddy tells me you might be able to sell them, get them out of my hair."

This time my smile was genuine, even though I didn't think my answer was going to be one he wanted to hear. "Oh, I'd love to help you, Mr. Watkins, but I'm afraid I'm not big enough yet to manage consignments. I just don't have the staff to keep track of whose stuff is whose and make sure everyone gets paid."

He stared at me for a minute before he shook his head and laughed. "No, girl, I don't want to be paid. I just want the stuff gone. I'd like to give it to you if that's okay."

I stared at him for a long second. "Well, my accountant says I need to be careful about gifts, so how about I pay you a little something for them outright? That way my books are in good order, and you can go out for a nice steak dinner or something."

Ace's face lit up even more. "Or I can put it in the gum fund. You would not believe how much I spend on gum."

"I bet I wouldn't," I said. "Do you have the things with you?"

"Most of it, but there are a couple of pieces, a thresher, an old plow, that I couldn't lift by myself. Maybe you and that sheriff of yours could come out and pick them up tomorrow?" He winked at me as he spoke in that way that people do when they feel like they've figured out a secret.

The fact that Santiago and I were dating wasn't a secret, but it had caused a bit of conversation in town. I looked at Mr. Watkins, managed to manufacture a little shy smile for his sake, and said, "Sure. If Santi isn't available, Dad can help."

For a split second, a flash of what looked like anger crossed Ace's face, but then he was back to smiling. "Sounds great. Maybe tomorrow afternoon after church?"

"Perfect. Now, let's see what you've got in that truck of yours." Ace had driven the same Chevy pickup since I'd been in high school. The bumpers were held on with wire, and the sides were rusting through but he made his way through town on his errands with no trouble, it seemed.

Now, he'd used that old beauty to bring me a treasure trove of goodies including more hand-held implements like the hook but also some impressive lengths of chain that I could see someone turning into rain chains and a couple of metal cages that had the prettiest patina and would look great hung in a corner with a trailing plant in them.

I climbed up into the bed and began handing the items down to Ace, but within a moment, Saul was there and taking over for the older man. I was glad for the help because while Ace wasn't complaining, he was looking a little peaked.

Soon, we had everything unloaded under the lean-to beside my shed, and Saul was ogling several fine pieces, including a pair of scythes that I knew would be a great addition to his farm implement collection in his own office. I made a note to give them to my landlord as a grand opening thank you and then turned my attention to thinking of an offer I could make Ace that would not be insulting to his generosity but also not undervalue the gift he was giving.

Within a few moments, I had settled on offering him a

hundred dollars. If he was anything like my dad, a hundred dollars would sound like a large sum, but it was also far less than what these items were worth. Dad had grown up dirt poor, and he wasn't much of a shopper these days . . . so he was really out of touch with the value of things today. When we'd bought my house, he had been astounded at the asking price. I figured, given that Ace was a generation older than Dad, he might have even more extreme impressions in that regard.

So I made my offer, and Ace shook my hand before saying, "That's two steak dinners for me and the Missus. And still a mighty hefty profit for you."

I blushed. Clearly, Ace was more up to speed on retail than my dad. "I'm happy to pay more," I said, hoping I hadn't insulted him.

"No, ma'am," he said. "I want to help you get this business off to a good start, and you really are saving me a bunch of trouble if I don't have to get someone out, especially when you take the bigger pieces tomorrow."

Saul looked from Ace to me. "Bigger pieces?"

Ace explained what he had in his barn, and I said Santiago and I would go out tomorrow to pick them up.

"One of my guys and I can go over right now and get them if you'd like, Ace," Saul said. "Save all of you the trouble and use our equipment to make it easier."

That same look of something crossed Ace's face before he said, "Well, that's mighty nice of you, Saul, but I want to be sure Paisley wants the things before she gets them. They might not be worth her trouble."

I studied his face for a second, and that tingly sensation moved from my back down to my fingers, but I nodded and agreed. It was really the least I could do given Ace's generosity, but also, if he was eager for me to get out to his farm, then I was almost as eager to get out there. With back-up of course. "We'll see you tomorrow then," I said as I shook the man's hand again. "I may just make you some cookies."

Ace shook his head. "Don't go to the trouble. The Missus got me off sugar twenty years ago. Best thing she ever did for me." He threw a hand up in the air as he got into the cab of the truck and pulled out.

Saul looked at me. "Well, isn't that something?" he said as he studied my face.

I met his eye. "Isn't it, though?"

I TEXTED Santiago as soon as Ace left and asked him to swing by if he had a minute, and he said he had just finished talking with Homer and would be over shortly with "refreshments." The winky emoji made me think I might enjoy these refreshments very much.

While I waited, I organized some of the things that Ace had brought over and made a list of what I needed – plants, crystals, bolt cutters – to finish displaying them the way I wanted. I had hung up the chains, but I thought adding a bit of shine with some quartz crystals might make them even more lovely for someone's garden.

By the time Santiago came with a six-pack of pumpkin cider, I had gotten Ace's things into an order that showed them off pretty well and was back to arranging Mika's offerings. "Hey, Beautiful," Santi said as he set down the drinks and came over to give me a hug.

"Hi, Handsome," I echoed. "How was everything?" My heart was racing even as I asked, but when he took my hand and led me over to the two metal lawn chairs by the front door for people who needed to wait for pokey shopping partners, he said, "It was good, Pais. I'm sorry about earlier. I was a little thrown."

"You have nothing to be sorry for. Seriously. You were doing your job, and my father was making your job harder. If anyone should be sorry, he should." I felt my anger with my dad cresting again.

"And he is. He apologized several times," he said as he reached over, braced the lip of a cider on the edge of the window sill, and popped the cap off before handing it to me. "Imagine if it had been Mika's father . . ."

I laughed. "Oh, I would have turned that wretched man in immediately." Mika's dad was an abusive, manipulating jerk, and if I could have any part in keeping him away from his daughter, I would do it in a heartbeat. Mika had told him over and over again that she didn't want to hear from him, but he didn't believe her. After all, how could she not want to have something to do with someone as wonderful as him?

But when I thought about it that way, the fact that my dad had simply been trying to take care of his friends made me able to hold a bit more grace for him. I took a deep breath, looked at Santiago, and nodded. "Good. Now what?"

"Now, I need to figure out how Leo Farrow died. All the men I talked to, including Ace Watkins and Melvin Smith, said Leo Farrow was dead when they found him. He'd been stabbed, they said. And so they just disposed of his body to keep his wife from suffering too much with a scandal." Santi had a furrow between his eyebrows, and I knew that look. He didn't buy that for one second.

"How exactly is it better for his wife that he just disappear, never to be heard from again, than to be found dead?" I tried to put myself in that situation, tried to imagine how I would feel if Santiago just went away; tried to picture myself if he was murdered. I couldn't dwell there long and both scenarios were horrible, but somehow the idea that he had just abandoned me seemed worse. Then, I'd have to recover from betrayal and loss, not just loss.

"I don't know. Is it better to realize the person who killed your spouse is in your community?" Santi sighed. "But either way, they covered up a crime. Maybe a crime one of them committed, maybe not."

"Right," I said. "So now you find out how Farrow died. How do you do that?"

Santiago shook his head. "I have no idea, but tonight, I'm just here to help you and get a little tipsy because," he glanced at his watch, "my shift just ended." He popped open another cider on the window and sat down next to me again. "What needs doing?"

"Well, actually, I need to tell you about my afternoon first. Can you clock back in for a second?"

Santiago groaned. "I suppose I can for you." He pretended to slip a timecard into a punch box and looked at me. "So what's up?"

"Ace Watkins came by today." I tried to sound nonchalant, but Santiago sat up immediately and put his drink down.

"Why?"

"He brought some things for me to sell." I stood up. "I'll show you." I walked him outside and pointed out the display of farm implements I'd created. "All really cool stuff."

I was doing my best to just speak factually, but I was itching to share my unease with the situation. I knew, though, that Santi needed to get the information first so he could form his own opinion. "And he has a couple of bigger pieces that he asked if you and I could pick up tomorrow afternoon."

This bit caused Santiago to raise one eyebrow. "Oh?"

I nodded. "Saul offered to go over with his crew and get them today, but Ace said he wanted me to see the items first to be sure I wanted them."

"And you didn't want to go with Saul this afternoon?" Santiago said.

I just looked at my boyfriend and waited.

"You think there was a reason he wanted you to go to his house?" he said.

"He specifically asked for you to come but didn't balk much when I suggested if you were busy Dad would come," I added.

"So it's you he wants out there."

"It could just be because he has a plow he wants to give me," I said with a twist at the corner of my mouth.

"Right? Clearly that's what this is — a man who was just linked to a nearly eighty-year-old murder suddenly is hit with a spark of generosity toward the granddaughter of one of the men involved. Surely, it's just coincidence." Santiago rolled his eyes so far back in his head that he could probably see the road behind him.

"He did say that Dad had mentioned that I was opening a shop, so that might have inspired him." I knew that sounded lame, but I'd found I did better when I thought the best of people, considered them as truthful until proven otherwise. Call me naïve, but I considered myself trusting . . . until I couldn't be anymore.

Santi kissed my cheek. "You are a sweet woman, but seriously, Ace Watkins is no doddering old man. He knew what he was doing coming here."

"So I guess you'll be coming with me tomorrow?" I winked.

"I wouldn't miss it . . . for many reasons." He winked back and then led me back inside. "Now, what needs doing?"

AFTER ANOTHER TWO HOURS, a delicious plate of pad Thai that we had delivered, and a couple of ciders, the storefront felt pretty much ready. I still had to set up the register, which would be delivered Wednesday, and my banners for beside the road would be ready later that day. But otherwise, the merchandise was set, and I loved it. Things looked rustic but cheerful, and Mika's pieces added just the right bursts of color to highlight her fine skills and set off the many tones of brown and gray on display.

When Santi and I drove out of the gate of Saul's lot and then locked it behind us, I felt great. I forced myself to let my nerves go, trust that the grand opening would be amazing, and sit in confidence that I'd discover anything further that needed doing.

I waved to my boyfriend as he turned the opposite way toward his house and put on a little Elephant Revival to sing me home. Their Americana folks sounds were just what I needed to close out a weird but ultimately good day.

In fact, I was so into my singing that it took me about two-thirds of the drive to realize that the same pair of headlights had been behind me as I wound my way through the backroads toward my house. They were the fancy lights, the blue-tinted ones, and I could see them turn a bit on the corners as they swung through the hills and valleys of the countryside.

In the movies, people always speed up when they're being followed, but then they run off the road, which is exactly what would happen here if I took any of these curves too fast. So I kept my pace and voice-texted Santiago. "I'm being followed," I said.

"Me, too," he answered. "Don't go home. Double-back. Meet me at Mika's."

I was almost at my driveway, but there was no way in the world I was leading whoever this was right to my dimly lit, rural homestead, not when the only guard on site was a grumpy Maine coon cat. I drove right on by, crossed the railroad tracks, and then took the first right back toward town as I sent another voice text to let Mika know we were on our way and ask her to open the shop.

"On it," she said, and as I turned into town, I could see the lights from her front windows blazing brightly. She was the only shop, besides the inn up the street, that looked open, and I was glad for the beacon of light as I sped up, jumped out of my car, and sprinted toward her door. Once inside, I turned back just in time to see a sleek sportscar pass on by without slowing down.

A moment later, Santiago came around the corner from the back alley. "Did you see the car?"

"Yep," Mika said. "Tesla SUV. Charcoal gray. Illegally tinted windows. No plates."

I stared at my best friend. "Wow. You know your cars."

"Just that one because it's what I'm going to buy when my online business takes off." She smiled. "What's going on?"

"Someone followed me home from the shop," I said.

"Same," Santiago added. "I saw the car pull by the alley, but it was too far away for me to get a make and model unlike Eagle Eyes here." He turned to me. "You okay?"

"Yeah, I am. I'm just glad Sawyer wasn't with me." I sighed and thought about how much more panicked I would have been with a three-year-old strapped into the backseat. "And I'm glad I noticed before I got home."

"Agreed," Santiago said, "and maybe if they followed you here, they don't know where you live. Maybe."

I groaned. "I'm going to have to be watched again, aren't I?" In the past, my penchant for finding bodies had meant I had to have police protection, and while I really appreciated the company of a particular police officer, I wasn't much in the mood to be observed twenty-four seven.

Santiago shook his head. "No, I don't think we need to do that. No direct threat has been made, and they followed me, too. But I'd feel better if you came to my house for the night."

I blushed, and I saw Mika grin before looking away. "I could always stay here with Mika," I said.

"No, I think Santiago is right. They saw you come here, so if whoever this is does want to hurt you, they'll come to find you here," Mika said.

"Which is why I'd like you to come to my house, too, Mika." Santiago's voice was firm enough to know that this wasn't a friendly request.

Mika drew in a breath that lifted her shoulders several inches and then sighed. "I'll be right back." She turned and went to the back of her shop and up the stairs to her apartment above. I watched as lights clicked off, and then, the store went mostly dark. She came out, locked the door behind her and said, "Ready for my first co-ed slumber party." She was trying to be upbeat, but I could hear the fatigue in her voice.

"You better have good snacks," I said to Santiago and followed him around the corner to his cruiser. I climbed into the back seat and smiled at him in the rearview mirror.

I had thought Mika would sit next to him, but instead, she got in next to me and closed the door. "This will hopefully be the only time in my life that I ride in the back of a police car, so make it worth my while, Officer," Mika said.

"Your wish is my command," he said and turned on the lights and the siren and took us screaming down Main Street. The few people out in town stared as we blew by, and Mika and I used our best prom queen waves as we zoomed by. By the time we hit the two-lane road just outside of town, Mika and I had created long rap sheets for ourselves that included crimes from "eating the last piece of cheesecake without asking if anyone else wanted it," "dosing our toddler with just a bit of Benadryl on a night when he had three bug bites and you really needed him to sleep," and something Mika described as particularly heinous, "knitting socks with worsted weight yarn." I had to take her word on that one.

We giggled all the way to Santi's house, and when we pulled up and he let us out of the back, I said, "You may regret this," as I kissed his cheek.

"*May*," he quipped and opened his front door. Santiago's house was gorgeous and comfortable, a craftsman bungalow that he had remodeled a bit to make the space feel more open. Even though he and I mostly hung out at my house because of the solitude and because Sawyer was often there, I had enjoyed several great meals at his spacious dining room table, and now, I plopped down in a chair at the side of the table and said, "Anyone up for Uno?"

Santiago rolled his eyes. "I was going to make chocolate popcorn. Interested?"

"Seriously? You have to ask?" Mika said.

Santi grinned. "Great. Why don't you two make yourselves at home in the living room, and I'll bring you your snack."

"What service!" Mika said with a wink at me.

It was only then that I remember Mika's date. It was only eight-thirty, so we hadn't even gotten to the nine p.m. check-in time. I winced as I turned to her. "Sorry, I forgot to ask earlier. The date didn't go well?"

I saw Santiago tilt his head in our direction just slightly. Clearly he was curious, too.

"Actually, it went very well. He packed a picnic, and we ate at the gazebo in town. But then, there was a food truck crisis with his daughter, and he had to rush off." She picked up her phone. "I should check to see how things are." She stood and walked out onto Santiago's back deck.

"A food truck crisis?" I said to the man who was concocting some amazing chocolate scent on the stove.

"Actually, it was. Jill had a flat tire right on the bypass in town. She panicked, and so her dad went to help." Santiago stirred the sauce in the pot. "He called me as soon as Jill was safe and the truck was towed out of the road. He was really sad he had to leave early."

I looked out the sliding glass door and saw Mika smiling and laughing with the phone to her ear. "Well, she doesn't seem to be upset."

"I expect not. She suggested they go up on the Parkway to

finish their picnic tomorrow. Chris was excited." Santiago said as he dripped dark brown chocolate over the popcorn he had just poured out of the bag. "He really likes her."

I glanced at my friend outside again. "Seems like she really likes him, too."

"Shall we?" Santiago said as he came over with the bowl of popcorn in his hand and offered me his other arm. "I was hoping maybe we could start *Manifest* together."

I grinned. I had been eager to watch this show for a while, but I knew he'd like it, too. So I'd waited. "Awesome. Just so long as we can agree to watch separately if we are so inclined."

"Agreed as long as we catch up to each other and watch some together, too." He leaned over and gave me a quick kiss. "It could be our show."

"Are you two talking about *Love At First Sight* because I am so down," Mika said as she came into the room.

"No!" Santiago and I said in unison. My best friend had the *worst* taste in TV shows. She loved all the ones about romance on secluded islands and people getting married without ever meeting. Fortunately, Santi and I were on the same page about that stuff. "*Manifest*," I said.

"Alright, twist my arm into watching Josh Dallas and J.R. Ramirez if you must," she said as she plopped down on the other side of me and put her hand into the popcorn bowl.

Santi looked at me. "Are those people from the show?"

Mika rolled her eyes. "Seriously, why do you people watch TV if not for the beauty?"

"That's a yes," I said. "But first, tell us what's up with Chris. Is your picnic still on for tomorrow?"

Mika blushed. "I guess he told you," she said to Santi. "Yes, we are still having our picnic tomorrow. He's picking me up right after church."

I smiled. "Awesome." Lately, Mika had been coming to church with me. Neither of us thought of ourselves as church types, but something about the folks at Bethel made us feel at home. And given that we'd just helped them with a major situation around their new building, we had gotten to know folks pretty well. "Mary's preaching you know?"

"She is?" Santiago asked. "Mind if I tag along?"

I grinned. "I know she'd love to see you there. And she tells me that the choir is working on something special, too." Mary Johnson had become a dear friend in the last few years, and when I'd started attending her all-black church, she hadn't hesitated to take the white lady under her wing and get me oriented. Now, I was just a part of the congregation with a slot to keep the nursery every six weeks just like the other volunteers. "Be forewarned, though," I told my boyfriend, "the ladies there like handsome men even more than Mika here."

Santiago rolled his eyes. "So noted. Now, I know the two of you have sewing on hand – I saw the bags – so why don't you get to that, and I'll keep working on this soapstone swallow that I may finish in time for Demetrius's Christmas present next year?"

Demetrius, another member at Bethel, and Santiago had become good friends recently, and the older man had taught Santi to carve the soft stone that he could dig up in old quarries just south of Octonia. Demetrius was very skilled, creating two-dimensional and three-dimensional pieces of art that reflected the mountains and the culture around us. Santiago was just learning, but I was pleased to see that what he had said was going to be a swallow actually looked pretty much like a bird at present. A bird with a huge head, but a bird still.

For the rest of the evening, the three of us worked with our hands and let ourselves disappear into the world of a plane that miraculously reappears after five and a half years, and I couldn't help but hope for a similar miracle when it came to solving a nearly eighty-year-old murder case.

6

The next morning, Mika and I both slept in. After luxuriating in the exquisite taste in sheets and mattresses that Santiago had for his guest rooms, we walked out into the living room to the smell of what could only be waffles.

Sure enough, there was Santiago in a pair of khakis and a polo flipping over one of those professional waffle makers that I had only ever seen at hotel breakfast bars in the past. Across the peninsula in his kitchen, he had set out sliced strawberries, whipped cream, maple syrup, and some of the most amazing looking sausage I had ever seen. Everything smelled wonderful, and it looked just as appetizing.

"If this is your normal morning," Mika said, "I'm happy to pay rent."

Santiago grinned. "You are welcome here anytime for my Sunday morning special." He looked at me and winked. "You, madame, are due for coffee. Two sugars, almond milk creamer. Mika, how do you take yours?"

Mika's eyes went wide as she said, "He knows about the almond milk switch."

I nodded. "He does. She'll take regular milk or half and half if you have it, no sugar."

"Coming right up." He popped a cup into his single-serving coffee maker and let it pour into a very cute mug that read, "Queen," before adding half and half and passing it to Mika.

"Do I want to know why you have a mug that reads, 'Queen?'" I asked with a playful tone but a genuine curiosity. Maybe this would be the moment I found out that Santiago had once been a major relationship that he hadn't told me about yet.

He served each of us a waffle and put one on a plate for himself before pointing to the bar and getting in line behind us. "This was my mother's way of praying for me to find the perfect woman."

Mika held the mug out. "Shouldn't Paisley have this one, then?"

He shook his head and smiled. "No, she has the mug she needs." I looked down at mine more closely and saw, written in a beautiful font just around the rim, "Your people will be my people."

I swallowed hard and pushed back the tears. Nothing could have said more about how Santiago felt about me than that. He had, from the get-go, taken to my people as much as I to me, especially Sawyer, and now that I thought about it, I was pretty sure that's why I'd let myself fall in love with him. If he loved my people, and my people loved him, then we were good. Very good.

I smiled at him and quietly took his hand under the counter as I waited for Mika to take a triple serving of whipped cream. Then, I kissed his fingers and helped myself to a load of strawberries, maple syrup, and then my own double-dose of whipped cream. As our friend from high school, Nikki, always used to say, "You got to eat big to get big, ya'll."

As we ate the delicious waffles – crispy on the outside and

soft as butter on the inside – the three of us chatted about anything but Leo Farrow's murder. I told them about how Mary was preaching on the definition of love as God sets it out and how I was excited to hear what she had to say. Mika told a story about how once a man had said he'd loved her and then, when she said she wasn't sure about him the next day, he'd sent her a note that said she just wanted to be miserable. "I don't think he knows what love means," Santiago said.

The rest of our conversation floated through the usual horror stories of romances gone wrong that single people have accumulated by middle-age. It was always good to lament our poor choices with good friends, and I was glad I didn't hear anything terribly brutal from Santiago, either in terms of what he said or had experienced. No one gets to mid-life without damage, I knew that, but if the man I loved had come through relatively unscathed, I was happy for myriad reasons.

After about an hour, we all worked together to clean up the kitchen, and then Mika and I donned the two dresses she had grabbed from her house the night before. I was glad she and I wore almost the same size because I really didn't want to go to church in my dirt-covered jeans and ratty T-shirt from the day before. I knew no one there would bat an eye and would welcome me gladly no matter what, but I still liked to look nice for services, especially since many of the older women in the congregation still donned hats and gloves for Sunday mornings.

Fortunately, my rubber sandals had just enough shimmer to them to look a bit metallic under the long maxi dress Mika had brought me, and since I didn't wear much make-up most days, I didn't think anyone would notice that I didn't put any on today. I slipped my usual headband on to push my hair back and cover the ponytail ridge from the day before and decided I was good enough for God and God's people.

The three of us rode in Santiago's civilian car, and this time

I sat in the front with Mika lounging across the back seat. We'd stayed up way too late sewing and watching four episodes of *Manifest*, and given how quickly Mika had taken to a prone position in the back seat and how heavy my eyelids were feeling, I hoped Mary's sermon was rousing so I didn't doze off. That would be both rude and humiliating.

But when we walked in, the organist was in his element with a rousing rendition of "Pass Me Not" that had me dancing a little as I headed toward my usual pew with Mika and Santiago right behind. Everyone around us waved or leaned forward or back to greet us as we sat down, and then I felt a heavy hand on my shoulder and turned to see Demetrius behind us. "Good to see all of you," he said and clapped Santiago on the back hard enough to force the man to huff out a burst of air.

"Good to see you, too," I said just as the choir began to join in and sing as they swayed and clapped their hands. Soon the entire congregation was up and on our feet, and while I was still pretty reserved with my movements, I managed to get a pretty good clap on as we moved through the verses. I was wide awake now.

After the announcements were over and a tiny boy from the congregation had said a heartfelt prayer for everyone who "had" to go back to school, Mary took her place behind the pulpit. She looked long and hard at all of us, a smile sitting softly on her lips. "It's good to see you all," she said.

A murmur of "Good to see you, too" spread through the sanctuary.

"I mean, really, just as you are, pain, beauty, questions, grief, profound joy, love – whatever you are carrying today, whatever doubts you have about how God feels about you, I am here as God's witness to say, God is happy to see you."

"Amen," a man in the back shouted.

"And not just here, friends, everywhere. Even if you never

make it to church another Sunday, even if you decided church isn't for you, even if you never darken the door of this building again, God is always, always glad to see you."

I sighed and felt something loosen in my chest as I settled into the truth my friend was sharing. I had stayed away from church for a long time because I couldn't carry the weight of the should and the "do more" that came with church, but here, I was reminded every week that God simply loved me, wanted the best for me, and was rooting for me all the time. It was a message I would never tire of hearing.

Santiago and Mika seemed absorbed in what Mary was saying, too, and I couldn't blame them. Who wouldn't want to be reminded that the Creator of the universe loved you? Plus, Mary was a charismatic speaker. She had the cadence of a great orator, and the congregation was beginning to stir with the joy and affirmation that always left me filled up with energy and hope after a service. The Amens were flying, and one woman in the front shouted, "Preach it, Girl." It felt good to be here. It felt like home.

When Mary's sermon was over, the choir started low and slow on a gospel rendition of "Troubled Water" by Simon and Garfunkel. When the chorus came, their voices broadened, and in that moment, I felt absolutely sure that God had me and would never let me go. It was glorious.

After the service, the sanctuary was humming with conversation and energy, and Mika, Santiago, and I made our way to the back of the church, where Mary was standing with the pastor to greet everyone. I gave her a big hug and said, "I needed that today. Thank you."

She smiled. "I needed it, too." Then she turned to Santiago and said, "Glad you could join us today." She hugged him, too, and then pulled Mika tight to her chest for an extra-long minute.

"See ya'll at lunch in a few?" she asked us.

I smiled. "You game?" I asked Santiago.

"That depends. Is there pot roast?" He grinned.

"You are in luck, sir. It's in the oven as we speak. And what about you?" she said to Mika.

Mika blushed. "I have lunch plans already, but thank you for the invitation."

I leaned forward and whispered in Mary's ear, "She has a date."

Mary's smile spread across her face. "I hope lunch is amazing, and I'll want a full report."

"You got it," she said and laughed. "I better get going." She looked up the street and saw Chris's Charger sitting on the curb. "See you later this afternoon?"

"Definitely. Let me know when you're back, and I'll come by," I said before looking at Santiago. "That plan works, right?" I didn't want to say anything in the midst of the crowd outside church, but I wanted to be sure Santiago thought it was okay for Mika to go home.

"Yep, we'll both go by. I'll need an update, too." He waved at his friend up the street and then said to Mika, 'Have a great time."

She smiled and jogged up the street. I so hoped she had a blast today. She deserved it.

I turned to Mary and said, "Mind if we head over and get the table set?"

Mary smiled. "Not at all. I'll be along shortly."

I took Santiago's hand and led him up the sidewalk and across the road to Mary's house. Her home was always so inviting with hanging baskets on the porch and a seasonal wreath on the door. I slipped my keys from my pocket and unlocked the front door, grateful that Mary, Mika, and I had all exchanged keys some months ago just in case.

Now, when I opened the door, the scent of onions and beef wafted through the air, and Santiago actually groaned. I decided not to tell him that the scent was only one-tenth as good as the taste. Mary was some kind of amazing cook.

I led the way into the kitchen, and we grabbed silverware and a stack of plates and set the long, mid-century table in the dining room with eight services. Mary never knew exactly how many people would come over, but she planned for as many as she could comfortably seat and then had extra ready for any overflow.

As he set out the assorted collection of dinner plates that Mary had picked up at yard sales over the years, he said, "Does Mary know about Farrow's body?"

I shrugged. "I haven't told her, but really, do we think anyone in town doesn't know?"

"Good point," he said with a small wince. "Some days it would be nice to live somewhere with a little anonymity."

I sighed. "Yeah, but then the love that Mary talked about might not be as tangible as it is here." I returned to the kitchen and came back with the cut-glass goblets Mary used for Sunday lunch and set one at each place. "Do you want to avoid the subject at lunch?"

Santiago folded orange cloth napkins and put them under each fork. It took a few minutes, and then he said, "Let's see if anyone knows anything about Farrow. But we won't bring up Salis and the other men who might have been involved."

I nodded. "I like that plan." I wasn't really worried about the men's reputations, but I didn't know if I could tolerate people dissecting my father's actions in front of me. Better to let that happen out of my earshot.

Once we had the table set, we returned to the front porch and sat in Mary's glider while we waited for folks to arrive. Within a few minutes, six folks, including Mary, had joined us on the porch, sitting in the rockers and on the railing as we talked about church and Mary's preaching ability.

After a few minutes, Mary announced that dinner was

ready, and I followed her inside to get out the food while
everyone else filled drink glasses with the sweet tea from
Mary's fridge before sitting down to eat.

Of course, the pot roast was amazing, melt in your mouth
and rich with flavor as were the carrots, onions, and potatoes
that went with it. A green salad made with ingredients from the
farm up the road made for a perfect meal. At least I thought it
was perfect until Mary pulled a glazed lemon Bundt cake from
the pantry and said, "One of Lucille's."

Everyone at the table groaned. My step-mother was infamous for her baked goods, and this was a classic recipe for her.
It was the perfect balance of sweet and tart and so heavy that it
felt like you gained a pound just from the weight of the cake
itself. But man, even if that was true, it was every bite worth it.

As everyone savored Lucille's cake, Santiago said, "So I
suspect all of you have heard that we found Leo Farrow's body
out at the barn on Friday?"

Everyone nodded, and Mary shot me a glance before
nodding herself. "Terrible thing," she said.

"Obviously, I'm investigating the crime, so I'm wondering if
you all know anything about what might have happened
there," Santi continued.

For a moment, everyone at the table looked at me, and then
all their eyes turned down to their plates as if they had been
choreographed. I sighed. Clearly, everyone knew more than
just about the body, and as clearly, no one wanted to upset me.

"It's okay, everyone. I know that my dad knew. I know that
his best friend, Homer Salis, knew, too. You won't be sharing
anything I don't already know or haven't at least considered." I
kept my voice steady but quiet, despite how nervous I felt.

Under the table, Santiago took my hand. "Anything you
might know or even have heard as a possibility would be helpful? And no one will know where I got my information. I'm not

interested in creating snitches. Just solving this case." Santiago had worked really hard to stay connected with all the members of our community, and his efforts had been especially hard with the black residents of Octonia because the previous sheriffs had unfortunately epitomized the stereotype of the racist cop.

Now, I was hoping that all Santi's efforts to gain trust had worked because more than anything, I wanted my dad to have clarity about what happened and to clear his name, too.

Mary looked up and smiled at me. "I don't know much, Pais, but what I heard was that four men killed Farrow for draft dodging." She took a deep breath.

"Did what you heard include the names of those four men?" Santiago asked.

Mary didn't take her eyes off me. "Yes." She then listed the same four names my dad had shared.

"Will telling me where you heard this information put someone else in danger?" Santi asked.

An older woman, Gloria, with long silver hair at the end of the table said, "It's not coming from one place, Sheriff. Everyone is saying it, been saying it a long time. Nobody knew where Farrow's body was, but everyone knew those men had killed him." She spoke with an assurance that made my blood grow a little cold.

"So it's common knowledge that Salis, Smith, Watkins, and Davis killed Leo Farrow?" I asked.

Every head at the table nodded. Then an elder from the church, Mr. Bates, said, "We all knew. Even back then. I was just a kid, but it wasn't a secret. Thing was, though, that they hid what they did well. Not the fact that they did it, mind, but how and where."

Mary added, "As I understand it, because no one ever found Farrow's body, police never pursued it as a crime."

"That's right," Mr. Bates said. "They just said he must have run off." He shook his head. "Everyone knew better, but what could we do?"

Santiago nodded. "Nothing. It wasn't your job to do anything, not your job to do anything now, either. Thank you for telling me what you know, and again, I won't say anything about our conversation. I appreciate your candor."

He squeezed my hand under the table. "And I appreciate the good food. Thank you for having me, Mary. Maybe I can return the favor sometime?"

Mary smiled. "I'd like that."

"Yes, thank you, Mary, and next week, I'm bringing lasagna, so don't you dare cook," I said as I stood up and carried my plate to the kitchen.

"That lasagna have spicy sausage in it," Mr. Bates asked. "I can't do spicy sausage."

I came back to the table and put my hand on his shoulder. "No sir. I make mine with spinach and lots of cheese, but no spicy sausage."

He put his hand on mine. "Good, good."

Santiago cleared his plate and then joined me at the door. "Thanks again," he said, and then we walked out the door and up the road to his car. After he shut the door he said, "So much for the theory that Farrow's widow didn't know he'd been killed, huh?"

"Sounds like everybody knew the truth."

Santiago said what I was thinking. "Even the police."

7

The drive out to Ace Watkins's farm took a few minutes, and as we rode, I tried to let the beauty of the fields along the drive capture me. The mountains out this way were wizened and curving, like an old woman's body, and I found myself wondering how much they knew, how much they could tell if they could talk.

The Watkins farm lay alongside a shallow, wide river that got its start in the mountains above, and with the water and the mountains along two sides of the property, it was about as beautiful a spot as I could imagine.

Today, though, I wasn't able to let myself get swept up in the beauty. I was too nervous about why we were out there in the first place. I knew there was more to this invitation than some old farm equipment, but what the *more* was, I couldn't say. And that had my pulse sprinting.

Santiago parked beside the large barn that sat just in front of the old stone farmhouse, and I stepped out and took a deep breath. The air was filled with the smell of cut hay and the slightest hint of manure, which for a country girl like me smelled just about perfect. The farm was immaculate with tidy beds for flowers by the house and black painted fences, some with hot wire behind them, for the goats and pigs in the pens. Chickens wandered freely while an old hound dog snoozed on the porch. It was the perfect painting of a farm if I ever saw one, and I felt some of my anxiety slide out my feet. Nothing that terrible could happen in a place this beautiful. At least I hoped not.

As we walked toward the house, Mr. Watkins came onto his porch and waved. "Glad you could make it. The equipment is back here in the run-in shed. Come on." He slung an arm over his head and turned beside the house, expecting us to follow. So we did.

When we got to the gray shed, I smiled. It was an antique pole barn with big, rough-hewn beams buried deep in the soil, and square-top nails driven through the boards. "This building is at least a hundred and fifty years old," I said.

"Two-hundred twenty actually," Mr. Watkins said. "It was built by the Pennsylvania Germans who came down. Just goes to show that when you take care of things, they last a long time." He patted his belly and gave me a wink.

I laughed. "So true," I said, trying to relax further now that we were talking about things I understood. Santiago smiled, too.

Mr. Watkins led us behind some huge stacks of hay and around the boxes of stuff that old farms simply seemed to accumulate. I was surprised how deep the building was until I realized it was built right into the hillside, a natural earth berm to keep the animals warm and cut down on material costs when building. It was genius.

There, at the back, I saw an old plow, but I was more distracted by the three folding chairs that were tucked into a corner. The old farmer pointed toward the chairs and then sat down in one himself. "When you leave, take that plow with you. We'll just say the thresher was too far gone to be saved."

I stared at him and then looked over at Santiago, who didn't look nearly as puzzled as I felt. "You need to tell us something, Ace?" he said.

My head pivoted from Santiago to Mr. Watkins. "You do?"

"I needed to be sure no one would hear." He swept his arm over his head. "We're secure here."

I glanced over at Santiago and saw a hint of a smile flash across his lips. He was enjoying the subterfuge, even if it was a little over the top. "Understood. What do you need us to know?"

Mr. Watkins leaned forward on his knees and folded his fingers together. "Melvin Smith killed Leo Farrow." His voice was clear as day, and the sound almost echoed in the small space. "I saw him do it."

I stifled a gasp and looked at Santiago who was nodding as if someone had just told him the special of the day was meatloaf. "Tell me what happened."

"Melvin was piping mad at Farrow and the other men who avoided going into that war. Said they were cowards and they put people like his nephew in danger because they didn't do their duty." Mr. Watkins sat back and sighed. "He needed to take it out on someone I guess."

I clenched my jaw and waited.

"That morning, he picked us all up—"

Santiago interrupted. "I'm sorry. Picked who up?"

"Oh, right. Me. Jimmy Salis, and Stephen Davis. He picked us up and said that he needed some help slinging hay. Given the season, a couple weeks later in the year than now, that made sense, so none of us asked any questions."

Santiago took the notebook out of his pocket and said, "Go on."

"We drove up past his daddy's fields, on up into the hollow, and the whole time I had a bad feeling. But I didn't say anything. Talk about a coward." He scrubbed a hand over his face. "When we pulled up to the Farrow place, Jimmy and I tried to stop him. We jumped out of the back of his truck and tried to talk some sense into him, but he wasn't hearing anything we was saying."

I looked up at the metal roof of the shed and let out a long slow breath.

"Stephen and Jimmy refused to go in, and I wanted to stay with them. But I thought maybe I could stop whatever Melvin wanted to do if I went with him. So I ran ahead and tried to warn Leo, but his wife said he was sleeping and wouldn't let me by." He shook his head. "I didn't want to push a woman, so I stopped. Stupid manners," he whispered.

Here, old-fashioned manners were everything. We still called people ma'am and sir, even if they didn't want us to. So I knew just what Mr. Watkins meant. That home training runs deep.

"Melvin was hell-bent, though. He pushed past her and charged into their bedroom. I ran behind him after helping Mrs. Farrow to her feet, but by the time I got there, it was too late. Farrow was dead on the rug, and Melvin was standing over him with the knife." Mr. Watkins' face had gone pale, and he seemed a little out of breath.

Out of that same impulse of politeness, I leaned forward and put my hand on his knee. "You okay?"

He looked down at me and nodded. "Better now that I've said it." He patted my hand.

Santiago sat forward and said, "What happened next?"

"Melvin rolled Farrow up in the rug, and I helped him carry him out the door." Mr. Watkins shook his hands. "I didn't know what to do, but I didn't want Mrs. Farrow to have to deal with his body."

I tried to imagine what I would have done in that situation, and while I hoped I wouldn't have gone this far, I decided not to judge Mr. Watkins. Clearly, he had lived with the guilt of this day for a long time, and I knew that he would have to face the legal consequences now. I imagined he knew that too and had wanted Santiago here for that very reason.

"So then what?" Santiago prompted.

"Then we put him in the truck and drove him back a ways to the old barn. We'd all played there as boys, and we knew about the privy hole. Knew, too, that no one much went out there."

"You dumped him and the knife there?" Santiago asked.

"Yes, sir. We did," Mr. Watkins said and then let out a long breath. His story was done.

I really didn't want to prolong this man's discomfort, but I still had a question, a very personal one. "How did my dad and Homer end up there?"

Mr. Watkins looked at me. "Did I not say that?" he asked. "They were there the whole time."

This time, I couldn't resist my gasp, and I turned frantically to Santiago, who was looking at me with sadness. He knew, just like I did, that my dad hadn't told us the whole truth. I felt like crying, but I forced myself to look at Mr. Watkins again and nod. "Thank you for telling us."

Mr. Watkins stood and turned his back to Santiago. "You can take me in now," he said as he forced his hands together behind his hips.

Santiago put a hand on his shoulder and turned him around. "That won't be necessary. You will have to be charged, but I don't have to arrest you. Just come down to the station tomorrow to make a statement, and we'll take care of things then. I don't think you're a flight risk, are you?"

Mr. Watkins actually smiled. "Not likely. Those pigs get mighty feisty if they aren't fed. We don't need them running wild."

I actually laughed at the idea of those giant, fat, pink pigs running loose in the mountains, and I felt a little of the unease in my belly loosen. "That would be a sight," I said.

"Would be, indeed," Mr. Watkins said with a chuckle. "Speaking of which, those baby goats are wily, and if they see a car in by their pen, they can be pretty crafty about getting out to jump on the hood. We better go check on them."

My boyfriend was a fast man when he needed to be, and as I watched him sprint ahead to be sure his cruiser hood wasn't dented by bouncing goat feet, I took the chance to talk with Mr. Watkins alone. "Can I ask you something, Mr. Watkins?"

"Of course, but only if you call me Ace. Mr. Watkins was my dad." He smiled at me. "You want to know what your dad knew, I expect."

I stared at him and then nodded once.

"Nothing, girl. Not a thing. He was just a little tyke, he and Homer both. They trusted their daddies, as boys should, and to their credit, Jimmy did everything he could to keep them from knowing what was going on."

"Everything but keep them from being there in the first place," I spat.

Ace put his arm on my shoulder and turned me toward him. "I know you're upset. And I understand why. But times were different then, and to be honest, Jimmy was doing more than most men did. His wife was busy with the little ones, and on Saturdays, when he wasn't working, he tried to give her a bit of a break by taking Homer with him everywhere. Lots of times your dad tagged along while we men went fishing. With his daddy away, we tried to help your granny out by including him."

Tears swam in my eyes as I thought about these men taking care of my dad. No wonder my dad was so quick to take care of Sawyer when I needed help. "I see," I said. The story didn't help me understand why my dad hadn't told us the whole truth, but at least it gave a reason why he was exposed to such a horrible thing. Not a good reason, mind you, but a reason.

I sighed and on impulse hugged Ace. He gave me a quick pat on the back and then pulled away. I was pretty sure I saw tears in his eyes before he hustled on up the hill toward the house ahead of me.

ON THE RIDE back to my house, Santiago stayed quiet, and while I had about a thousand questions, most pressing of which was what this information meant for my dad, I didn't say a word either. He clearly needed to gather his thoughts, and I knew that pressing him now would only frustrate both of us.

When we got to my house, I went upstairs to change my clothes, and I heard Santiago making tea in the kitchen. As I came down the stairs, he handed me a mug and pointed toward the front door. I led the way to the swing on the front porch, and when he sat down next to me, he said, "You okay?"

I sighed. "I don't know. How about you?"

"I am, but this isn't about my dad. What do you want me to do?" he asked quietly while he looked out over the field below us.

I stared at him for a moment. "You need to do what you need to do as the sheriff," I said firmly. "My dad is a big boy. He made his choices."

Santiago reached over and took my hand. "You know it's not that simple, Pais." He put my fingers to his lips. "Your dad is in a tough situation, one he didn't create for himself."

I sighed and then inhaled deeply. "I know. But he has always told me to tell the whole truth."

"And nothing but the truth?" Santiago said with a small smile.

"He did; always like *Perry Mason*," I said. "I just don't understand why he didn't tell us everything."

"Maybe it's time we asked him that," Santiago said just as I heard tires crunch on the driveway.

I stood and leaned around the side of the house to see my dad and Lucille parking. "You asked them to come over?"

"I hope that was okay. I needed to talk to him, and I figured you did, too. Thought maybe it was better if we both got it over with." He leaned over and kissed my cheek before walking down the steps to meet my dad with an outstretched hand. "Thanks for coming."

Dad and Lucille followed him back up on to the porch, where each of them took a rocker as Santiago sat back down next to me. "I heard you talked with Ace," Dad said as soon as he'd turned his rocker to face us.

"We did," I said. "And we learned that you know more than you've shared." I didn't even try to keep the knife out of my tone.

Dad furrowed his brows and looked at me. "What did he say?"

"He said you were there at the Farrow place when Leo Farrow was killed," Santiago said. "Is that true?"

Dad sat back and pushed his rocker back and forth for a few moments before he said, "I don't know."

I stared at my father. "What do you mean you don't know? Either you were there when a man was murdered or you weren't. How can you not know that?" My voice was getting louder, and I only kept from shouting because Santiago rubbed a hand over my knuckles.

"I mean I don't know. I can't remember everything from that day. Just bits and pieces," Dad sighed and massaged the back of his neck. "I've tried, but I really can't remember."

Lucille looked at me and said, "You know, Paisley, that sometimes traumatic events make us forget." She studied my face. "I expect you've had that experience."

I took a deep breath and thought back to the last few

months of my marriage, when my husband's behavior had gotten erratic as his drinking had gotten heavier. I had a few very specific memories from those days, but I also had lots of blanks, lots of places where the memories felt fuzzy or like snapshots instead of films. I inhaled deeply again and nodded.

"Your dad," Lucille looked at my father and then continued, "has lots of memories like that from his childhood."

I could tell there was a lot more to that sentence than my stepmother was saying, but I also knew she would let my dad say what he wanted now that she'd helped bridge the communication gap between us.

"Really, Dad? Was your childhood bad?" Dad didn't talk about his early years much except to tell funny stories about life on the farm or the time a wild boar chased him through the woods, but since we had regularly seen my grandparents, his parents, when I was a kid, I had assumed everything was okay with them, not perfect maybe, but good generally. Like it was with my dad and me.

"I wouldn't say it was bad," my dad said, "but some things were hard." He looked at Lucille. "Your papa wasn't an easy man to please, and your granny, she was too sweet for her own good sometimes." Dad swallowed. "And that's all I'm going to say about that."

I looked from him to Lucille, and she sighed. Clearly, there was a lot more here, but for now, we had to deal with the situation at hand. "Okay, so you don't remember that day completely?"

Dad shook his head. "I don't. I have a very clear picture of us in that barn and the rug, and I remember knowing something really bad was happening. But I really don't know if I knew what had happened or even if I had been at the Farrow place." He looked at me. "But if Ace says I was, then, I suspect he's right."

"Okay," Santiago said. "But if you can't remember, do you think Homer can?"

Dad sighed. "I don't know. I've always been afraid to ask. But maybe." Dad took out his phone. "Mind if I invite him over?"

"Seems like it might be a good idea," I said. "I'll order in some barbecue, slaw, and hushpuppies." We had this new barbecue place just up the road, and I'd been dying to try it out. Now seemed like as good a time as any, especially since they delivered. "Dr. Pepper okay for everyone?"

The three other people on my porch nodded, and I went inside to place our order, and to gather my thoughts. It was a big thing to absorb that my dad hadn't experienced the great childhood I had, but I also realized that the fact he had worked so hard to give me a good one meant even more now.

When I went back out to the porch after placing an order for two dozen hushpuppies, a pound of pork barbecue, a pound of brisket, and a pound of coleslaw, the mood was much lighter. Dad was telling Santiago the infamous wild boar and the shortcut story, and Santiago was laughing at the image of my dad being chased by a pig through the woods.

Lucille stood as I approached and said, "Show me your garden?"

I slipped my hand through hers and led her around the house. As we wandered through the gate into the garden, Lucille slipped her hand over mine on her arm. "He's never told you."

Without looking at her, I shook my head. "Not even enough for me to know what you're talking about."

She sighed. "Your grandfather's idea of discipline sometimes involved a beating with an axe handle."

I gasped and dropped my arm. "What?! He beat Daddy?" Tears were already on my cheeks.

"Your father doesn't call it beating. He calls it 'spanking.'"

She made air quotes with her fingers. "But yes, he was beaten. Often, it seems."

I put my hands over my mouth. "I can't . . ." All I could think was that I was glad my grandfather was dead because there was no way I could face him after learning that.

"Apparently, it was a very dark house, but your dad doesn't like to dwell there, doesn't like to think it affected him much or at all. He believes it's all in the past, not something that he needs to deal with now." From the tone of Lucille's voice, I could tell she didn't agree with my father, but she knew as well as I did that my father was the most stubborn of men when it came to something he didn't want to do, especially if it involved his health.

I nodded. "That's why he doesn't remember," I said matter-of-factly, but I didn't add that this was also probably part of the reason that Ace and the other fathers took Daddy with them so much. They just wanted to give my dad a break from all the darkness at his house.

"Right. He can't remember, and he doesn't really want to, I think." Lucille plucked a Roma tomato from the vine. "At our age, I can't really blame him."

I pulled out the front of my T-shirt and began filling it with tomatoes. "I guess, but in this case . . ." I was torn between wanting to help Santiago solve this murder and wanting to protect my dad, at least from his memories.

"In this case, your father is trying, Paisley. He keeps running through that day, and I expect he may uncover more. But maybe not." She dropped a handful of cherry tomatoes into my shirt and then headed toward the okra.

"Right. And maybe Santiago doesn't need more. If Dad thinks it was possible he was there, then maybe that's enough to corroborate Ace's story." I was hoping, anyway.

"I'm actually hoping that maybe Homer will return your father's kindness and fill in some of the gaps for all of us." She placed a huge handful of way-too-big okra into my shirt. "Here he is now, in fact."

I looked over at the drive and saw Homer's truck pull in and behind it another car was coming up the driveway. At first, I thought it was the barbecue delivery, but then I recognized Mika's face and saw Saul in the passenger's seat. I hoped I'd ordered enough food.

"Sorry to just drop by," Mika said as she jogged over. "I didn't realize other people would be here, but Saul and I were curious about what Ace Watkins had to say."

I gave her a hug. "Happy to have you. One sec." I stepped around her and hugged Homer Salis. "Thanks for coming, Uncle Homer."

"I figured it was time we talk all this through." He smiled at me. "Plus, I heard there was barbecue."

Just then, a sleek sportscar came down the lane, and it took me a minute to realize that this was our delivery driver. When the man stepped out, I did a double-take. He was about my dad's age with a perfect cut to his silver hair and cufflinks on his collared shirt. This was not the typical delivery person.

"Got a delivery for Paisley Sutton," he said as he handed me two bags of food. "Threw in an extra pound of barbecue on the house."

I studied his face and then his car. This was the Tesla that had followed me the day before, but I didn't know the driver. "Well, thank you," I said, "but please let me pay for the extra food." I wasn't sure what was going on, but I didn't trust the gift.

"Melvin!," my dad said as he came across the yard. "You take a demotion at the restaurant?" He shook the man's hand.

"Nope, just saw who the delivery was for and wanted to make your daughter's acquaintance. Melvin Smith," he said as he stuck his hand out to me. "I've known your dad since we were in T-ball."

I stared at my dad, and he made the slightest nod with his

head before saying, "Best runner on the team as I recall," he said with a laugh that I knew was forced but probably sounded genuine to everyone else. "Join us for dinner?"

"Well, if I wouldn't be imposing, I'd like that." He stepped over to Homer and shook his hand, too. "Good to see you, Homer. Got quite a reunion here." The men headed across the yard to the porch.

Dad turned back and said, "Paisley, if you and Lucille want to get us set up, I'll send Santiago and Mika in to help." He met my gaze and held it. Dad was already thinking I needed to give them a heads up.

"Sounds good," Lucille said before grabbing my arm and tugging me toward the side door. "Well, this definitely just got a whole lot more interesting."

8

As soon as Santiago and Mika came in the door, he said, "Your dad said you needed some help with the food."

I nodded. "Actually, he is just giving me a way to tell you that's Melvin Smith."

Santiago spun his head back toward the door he had just come through. "That man is not old enough to be Melvin Smith."

"It's his son, I expect," Lucille said. "He and Lee were friends as children."

Santiago sighed. "So the afternoon just got a whole lot more complicated?"

Mika groaned.

"Seems so," I said as I walked over and gave each of them a hug. "Now, if only Ace Watkins showed up, we'd have representatives from three of the family's involved."

"Funny you should say that," Santiago said as he grabbed the plates and napkins and headed toward the front door. "Your dad just invited him over."

I groaned. "Lucille, any brilliant ways to stretch food for

four to food for nine?"

"Oh, we can figure something out. Next trip, take these beers will you?" she said to Santiago.

"Got it." He walked out the door and returned for the beer. "This will hold them a bit. Be right back." He picked up the two cold six packs Lucille had pulled from the fridge.

"Now, let's see what we can add to this meal," Lucille said as she opened the fridge again.

Mika and Santiago made trips in and out with various trays and utensils, and within a few minutes, Lucille had made a relish tray with pickles, olives, and a pile of capers that I had bought on a day I was feeling adventurous about pasta. Then, we piled hamburger buns on a plate for those who wanted sandwiches instead of plain barbecue. A bowl of baby carrots finished off the meal, and I felt like at least people would have enough to fill their bellies before they left.

We carried the rest of the food out and set it on the folding table Santiago had set up by the side of the porch. Ace Watkins had arrived, and he was sitting on the swing beside Homer. It was kind of a quaint site, these two older men swinging away like school kids.

As soon as we declared the meal ready, the men insisted we go first, those Southern manners at work again, and Lucille and Mika and I helped ourselves to full plates before perching on the side of the porch, where Santiago soon joined us. We all ate quietly for a while, and the food was delicious. The brisket was smoky and tender, and the hushpuppies were the perfect blend of crunchy on the outside and soft on the inside.

Apparently, the scent was so enticing that even my cat, Beauregard, decided he needed to check it out, and for a bunch of "animals are animals" types, these old men sure loved watching a cat eat barbecue from a fork.

Soon, though, the food was gone, all but the capers, which I could completely understand since I hadn't even been able to

bring myself to cook with them, and everyone had compli-
mented Mr. Smith on his restaurant's food.

All pleasantries done, Santiago decided to take the lead.
Since we'd invited Homer and then Ace here and weren't clear
on what Melvin wanted, Santiago started with him. "Mr. Smith,
you probably heard about the body of Leo Farrow that was
found out on the old octagonal barn site earlier this week." His
tone was brisk, professional, and I found myself smiling as I
watched him do his thing.

"I believe I did hear something about that, yes." Melvin said
with what was clearly a false casualness. "Didn't you find it, Ms.
Sutton?"

"Actually, I did," Mika piped up. "That and the bloody
knife." Saul scooted his camp chair a bit closer to his niece.

"That's right," I said. "Santiago and I were there when she
found it. Does that matter?"

Melvin shrugged. "I doubt it, unless it means you're looking
for stories about things that don't need stirring up." He spoke
with a smile, but there was weight to his words.

"You mean, like a murder?" Santiago said, his voice sharp.

"What in the world are you talking about, Sheriff? Who said
anything about a murder?" Smith said.

"I did," Ace said from his seat on the swing.

"And I did, too," Dad added.

"They know, Melvin," Homer added. "We're here to come
clean. If you don't want that, then I suggest you go."

"Actually, Mr. Smith, at this point, I'm going to need to ask
you to stay. Why exactly are you here?" Santiago said as he
stood up and waited for Melvin Smith's answer.

The smile was gone from Smith's face. "I just heard Ms.
Sutton here was getting into the muck as she often does,
bringing up things that belong in the past. Wanted to be sure
she understood my family wanted no part of it?"

"That a message from your daddy, Melvin," Saul asked with a sneer. "Or just your cowardly usual?"

Melvin glared at Saul. "Should have known you'd be messed up in this revisionist nonsense, too, Saul. Always were too eager to make trouble."

I watched as Saul clenched his fists and then slowly stretched his fingers.

"This is a murder investigation, Mr. Smith," Santiago said as he took a step closer to the man. "I will ask any questions and do any muck stirring that needs to be done to solve this case." He shot a quick look at Ace Watkins, and I wondered what the plan was here.

"Well, you just leave my family out of it. We are good, upstanding members of this community, and we don't need our names dragged through the mud. My daddy has worked for this county for most of his life, and I won't let you ruin his reputation." Melvin stood up so quickly that the rocker bounced back against the house.

"I'll be needing to talk to him, Melvin," Santiago said. "Please let him know that he can either come by the station tomorrow or I'll be out to see him. In my police cruiser."

Melvin spat on the porch floor as he stalked toward the stairs. "We'll see what our lawyer has to say about that." He stomped down the steps toward his car.

"Thanks for the barbecue," Lucille yelled cheerfully.

A quiet chuckle passed through the rest of the gathering, and I stood up and said, "Who wants chocolate pudding cake?"

"Is that even a question that needs an answer?" Saul said as he stood and walked me to the door. "Let me help."

Saul was a very generous man, a giving man, but a traditional man. I had never once seen him do more than carry dirty dishes into the kitchen. Cooking, much less baking, was not something I imagined him doing. But I took the help and headed in.

Hot fudge pudding cake is one of those desserts that I always kept the ingredients for, just in case Lucille didn't bring along one of her amazing baked confections. Flour, sugar, cocoa, salt, and milk . . . all mixed and then put into the pan to bake. The cake parts rise to the top, the fudge parts sink to the bottom, and you have a gooey hot mess in a matter of minutes.

This time, Saul helped by sitting at the kitchen table and talking with me about my dad and this situation. I actually appreciated this form of help since tonight my nerves were so frazzled that I really needed to be able to move freely in my space without worrying about running into anyone. Plus, company was nice, as was what Saul was trying to do.

"He's always been sorry about that day, Paisley. You need to know that," Saul said as I measured flour into a bowl. "He told me about it. He was scared, wasn't sure what to do. It's one of my earliest memories, too."

I sighed. "So why didn't he tell someone, an adult?"

Saul shook his head as I poured the sugar into the bowl. "Homer didn't want his dad to get into trouble." He sighed. "Looking back, it seems obvious what we should have done, but we were just a bunch of scared kids. Your dad had more reasons to be afraid than most."

I turned toward him. "What do you mean?"

"You don't know?" When I shook my head, Saul said, "Your granddaddy and Jimmy Salis were best friends."

I dropped my head back. "So Dad was worried he'd get beaten if he got Jimmy Salis in trouble."

Saul rubbed a hand across his chin. "That's what I always figured." He stood up and came over to put an arm around my shoulder. "I saw the bruises your daddy had on his legs. I can't blame him for not wanting to get it worse."

The sorrow over my dad's hard childhood was swelling in me as I slid the bake into the oven. "Thanks, Saul."

He gave me a quick hug, but then the front door swung

open.

"There's been an accident just up the road, Pais. You have a first aid kit, right?"

I ran into the laundry room and grabbed the large bag I kept full of gauze, creams, and even a stitch kit for Sawyer's inevitable injuries. "Here. I'm coming, too. You might need more hands."

Lucille and Dad were already in their car, and I jumped into the front seat of Santiago's cruiser as we sped out the drive and toward the east. "Is it bad?"

Santiago shot me a look. "The person who called it in said she thought the man was seriously hurt."

I nodded and then looked at my boyfriend. "What aren't you telling me?"

"She said he was driving a silver Tesla." He sped up as we crested the hill I called Sawyer's tummy tosser, and we saw the cars on the side of the road. Melvin Smith's Tesla was rammed into the bank at the side of the road.

Santiago slid to a stop behind the car and turned on his lights. "Check with the witness," he shouted as he grabbed my first aid bag and sprinted toward the car.

I jogged up to the woman who was cradling the head of a young girl against her hip. "Are you guys okay?" I said.

"We're fine. We just saw it happen and wanted to be sure someone was here before we left." She looked like she was close to tears, but I knew she would do all she could to maintain her composure as long as that little girl was nearby.

Just then, Lucille and Dad pulled up and parked up the road. Dad put on a yellow safety vest he kept in the glove compartment in case Lucille got a flat tire and had to wait by the side of the road for AAA. Then, he began to direct traffic from the middle of the road.

Lucille came over to us and said, "Honey, my name is Lucille. Do you want to go sit in your car with me while your mom talks with my friend Paisley?" Lucille was always good at reading a situation. "If it's okay with your mom, I have some crackers and ginger ale in my purse."

The little girl looked up at her mom. "That sounds like a good idea, honey. I'll be right there." With another nod from her mom, the girl took Lucille's hand, and the two of them walked up the median to where the gray sedan was waiting.

"Can you tell me what you saw happen?" I asked the woman.

"I don't really know. I saw him coming down the hill back there," she pointed at the small rise behind us in the series of tiny hills on this strip of the road. "I didn't see anything unusual, but then he crested this hill and careened right into the bank. I don't think he even tried to stop himself." The tears were now pooled in her eyes, so I put my hand on her arm.

"Thank you for stopping. The sheriff has it in hand, and look, there comes the ambulance. Do you mind giving me your number in case the sheriff needs any more information?"

The woman shook her head and then reached into her purse for a pen and a receipt onto which she scribbled her name and number. "I'm happy to help any way I can."

"You already have," I said and gave her a quick hug before walking her back to her car.

After making sure that mother and daughter had made it out onto the road safely, thanks to Dad's surprisingly good abilities to direct traffic, I went to see what the situation was at Smith's Tesla. Given that I didn't see him out of the car, I guessed things were not good, and when the EMTs loaded their stretcher back into the ambulance and pulled away a few minutes later, I knew they weren't good at all.

"He's dead," I said when Santiago stepped back from the car and came to the shoulder.

"He is," Santiago said as he leaned against his cruiser's

trunk. "I don't see any brake marks, so it doesn't look like he even tried to slow down."

I told Santiago what the witness had said that confirmed his suspicions. "She said he didn't even look like he tried to stop."

"Which means he was either dead already or at least unconscious when he hit the bank." Santiago studied the car. "The coroner will have to determine that."

I nodded. "Either way, though, it seems odd that he wasn't conscious on the road. He didn't seem tired to you, did he?"

"No, he didn't, which has me worried."

"You think someone dosed him with something," I said. "At my house."

Santiago studied my face. "Maybe. But we don't know anything yet." He pulled me to him for a few moments before saying, "Here comes Savannah. She can take over directing traffic. I suspect you have a few folks with questions back at your place. Why don't you let your dad and Lucille drive you back?"

"You'll come when you're done?" I asked.

"Of course. See you soon." He kissed my cheek and then turned to direct his deputy and the coroner, who had also just arrived.

I joined Lucille at their car, and as soon as Savannah donned her own vest and stepped into the road, Dad joined us. "Ready to get back home?" he said.

I nodded. "Yeah, I guess." I sat in the back seat and rested my head against it. While I was glad Sawyer wasn't coming home until tomorrow, I really wished he was here. I could use a good snuggle and a belly laugh about now, and my kid was good for both.

Tonight, though, I had to settle for a bunch of old men who were, despite their good intentions, not really great at snuggles or belly laughs, at least not presently. Somehow, Saul had convinced all the men to remain at my house, probably by offering the last of my beer, and when we pulled up, Homer,

Ace, and Saul were all sipping their cold cans on the porch, and Mika had a glass of white wine.

I was thrilled to see, though, that they had picked every-thing up while we were gone, and when I had my own wine, I asked Mika if she'd been left to do it all. "Actually, no, although I was prepared for that," she said. "Ace is actually really good at washing dishes, and Homer made a batch of fresh whipped cream for the cake when everyone gets back. And apparently, even Uncle Saul had paid enough attention to know when to take the cake out of the oven. It was a team effort."

"Ye of little faith," Homer said as he took a swig from his beer. "We can be helpful, you know."

"We just don't choose to be when women will pick up the slack," Saul said with a grin as he raised his forearm to block my playful blow.

Once the joking settled down, the quiet came in heavy, and Ace asked, "So was the person okay?"

I shook my head. "No, he wasn't." I took a deep breath. "It was Melvin Smith."

Mika gasped, and the three men stared hard enough at me to make me feel like I was being weighed down by their gazes. "He may have been unconscious when he had his accident, I added before I explained what Santiago and the witness had said about Smith's driving.

Everyone around me looked at everyone else, and I could feel the webs of suspicion winding through the air. We all knew what this meant. Someone here had slipped Smith something.

I knew that it was not Saul or Mika, no question, so that just left Ace and Homer, one man who was my dad's best friend and one man who had told a really convincing story about Farrow's death just hours ago.

I tried to act nonchalant and said, "Santiago thinks it could have been a heart attack or aneurism or something. He'll be back soon to give us more of an update." I didn't sound convincing to my own ears, but both Ace and Homer seemed to relax a little.

Mika shot me a look, and I knew she didn't believe one thing I was saying. But we'd been friends long enough for her to know I only lied when I thought it was absolutely necessary. "You guys waiting here?" she said to the two older guys on the swing.

The men looked at each other, shrugged, and said, "Nothing better to do."

Mika stood. "I'll run up to the market and get some more beer then. Any requests?"

"I wouldn't turn down a Snickers if they have one," Saul said.

"Saul, we have hot fudge pudding cake to eat!" Mika said as she smacked his shoulder.

"Trust me, I can handle both," he said.

"Be back in a minute," she said as she rolled her eyes. She put on a good show, but I knew that candy bar would be in her hands when she got back.

As soon as the men started talking about their plans for hunting season, Lucille, Mika, and I excused ourselves to go plate the cake. It was best hot, and so that meant we needed to serve it soon. Besides, neither of us cared one iota about where the best tree stands were and who had what permit. Dad and Saul didn't care much either, but since they'd grown up here, they could both talk the talk right well, especially if it meant our two suspects would stick around long enough for Santiago to get back.

Fortunately, he wasn't long in coming, and when we came back out to the porch with cake and whipped cream for each of the men, he was already sitting on the porch. I served the older guys first and then plated some for him and Mika, who had just come back with two twelve packs of the grossest beer I could imagine. Given the men's positive reaction, though, they seemed pleased.

Each of them cracked open a fresh can and settled back to enjoy their cake from their laps. Sometimes I wished I lived a more cosmopolitan life with white tablecloths and two forks at fancy restaurant tables, but most of the time, I was happy to be surrounded by people who didn't bat an eye when you served them on a porch swing and gave them cheap beer.

Still, I wasn't completely at ease because, despite my lie about a natural cause for Melvin's death, the worry lines in Santiago's forehead made me think that wasn't exactly what we were talking about here. I waited for his lead, though, before I said anything else about the accident.

When the clatter of forks scraping against plates to get the last swirls of chocolate subsided, Mika and Lucille gathered up the plates, passed out more beer, and headed inside to do the washing up. I'd have to thank them later, but for now, I was just grateful to be a part of the conversation that now seemed inevitable.

"Gentlemen, we have to wait for the autopsy to be sure, but it looks like Melvin Smith was poisoned." Santiago turned to each man. "This afternoon."

9

I don't know what I expected – a quick confession, a brash denial, blows between the two suspects – but instead, Ace and Homer just nodded when Santiago mentioned poison and said something to the effect, "How terrible" and "That's too bad." To say they underreacted would be, well, an understatement.

But given that my dad almost always underreacted to nearly everthing, I wasn't as surprised as I might have been. It seemed to be a facet of the personalities of some rural men to take anything in stride, at least in a public setting. My dad had been known to fly off the handle and punch a wall or two in his younger years, but only rarely and only ever in the privacy of his own home.

Now, it seemed like Ace and Homer had received the same stoic training my dad had received, some sort of lesson about acting strong and tough no matter what, I imagined. In this case, though, it looked far more like acting or downright lying than it did some macho nonsense.

"Either of you know what might have happened?" Santiago asked.

The two men stared at the sheriff and then looked at each other. "I think he suspects one of us," Ace said.

"Seems he does," Homer added. "Sorry, Sheriff, you're barking up the wrong old trees here." He stood and stretched before picking up his two beer cans. "I best be off though. Need to feed the cat before she climbs the roof and gets onto my bed through my window again."

I stared at my dad's best friend and then glanced over at my dad, who had a very puzzled expression on his face. But when he didn't say anything, I didn't either.

"Well, if either of you think of anything," Santiago said as he rose to his feet, "You'll call me right?"

"Sure thing, Sheriff," Ace said as he stood, too. "And I'll be down tomorrow to give my statement on that other matter."

Homer glanced at the older man but didn't say anything. "See you at lunch tomorrow, Sheriff."

I glanced over at Santiago, who kept his gaze leveled on the two men as they walked across the yard. "Looking forward to it."

Once the men were in their cars and pulled out, I turned to Santiago, "What was that?"

"That? That was two men with a pact," Dad said.

"A pact?" I asked. "What do you mean?"

"Just trust me, Pais. Those men made a promise to each other this afternoon, and they aren't going to break that promise if they can help it." Dad dragged himself to his feet. "I'll help any way I can, Santi, but that's a mighty hard stone wall you're facing."

"I can be a bit of a jackhammer when I need to be, Lee. Don't you worry." He shook Dad's hand and then sat down again beside me on the porch floor. "This all just got a lot more complicated."

I sighed and leaned my shoulder against his. "When doesn't it get more complicated?"

"When you die," Saul said and followed my dad inside.

AFTER EVERYONE ELSE LEFT, I decided I wanted to give the house a good once over before Sawyer came back the next morning. Nothing was harder in terms of cleaning than trying to vacuum a house when your toddler kept unplugging the machine.

I apologized to Santiago that I wasn't much for sitting around and thinking anymore but that I didn't mind if he did, and he said, "Are you kidding? I couldn't sit still if I wanted to. Give me a dust rag."

So for the next two hours, we organized toys (and claimed a few for Goodwill), vacuumed, dusted, and even cleaned the kitchen and bathroom. By the time we were done, the house looked and smelled amazing, and Beauregard was thoroughly annoyed by the commotion. He seemed to get over it, though, when I sat down, turned on the TV, and picked up my sewing basket while Santiago took out his phone and began a new game of Words with Friends with my step-mom. They were fierce competitors, and I didn't dare interfere in their battle.

My eyes were tired, and it had been a long day. But I wanted to make progress on Father Winter, and so I took out the hoop, made a goal to finish at least two ten-by-ten squares and set to work. Once his game was done, Santiago turned on *Manifest*, and I actually managed to finish three squares while we binged through two episodes of our new favorite show. The mystery was getting intense, and I found myself wishing that I got "callings" that led me to help. Maybe if I did, I could help Santiago find who had killed Melvin Smith, Junior.

I wanted to ask him a million questions about the case, but I knew that both of us needed to let it rest for the night, let our minds work on things behind the scenes so that we could sleep.

. . .

THE NEXT MORNING, I woke at seven and texted Sawyer's dad to
ask him to bring him to my new shop at ten. I wanted to get an
early start on work, and I knew Sawyer would love helping me
as well as playing on the big equipment in Saul's lot.

When Saul had offered me the space, he had stipulated that
rent was only to be comprised of Sawyer visits and occasional
baked goods. So after giving my boy a big hug, hearing a bit
about his camping adventures, and being sure he had eaten a
good breakfast ("Two waffles, Mom," he assured me), I made
good on my rent and walked him over to see Saul.

My son had gone through all the usual phases of being
afraid of strangers and friends alike, but now he was in one of
those delightful developmental moments where he loved the
people he knew and was always excited to see them. Today
was no exception and as soon as the two spotted each other,
they grinned and ran to meet like they were in some
romantic movie on the beach. Only with gravel and construction dust.

Saul scooped Sawyer up and spun him around, and I
wished I'd pulled out my camera because this was precious
blackmail material for the future. The moment ended too
quickly for me to film, however, and soon they were headed my
way with what I could already tell was a request.

"Mom, can I go with Uncle Saul to his contruckton site? He
needs my help." Saw's vocabulary was amazing, but his
pronunciation always won the day.

"Sure, Saw, you can go to the contruckton site. Text me the
address and I'll pick him up in a couple of hours. We have a
hamburger date, remember?"

"Hambooger, Mom. You don't say it right," he said seriously.

"Alright, there, Mr. Know-It-All. Have fun," I said with a
laugh, "and don't forget to wear your hard hat."

"Already in the truck," Saul said as the two headed off to
Saul's pickup, where he had installed a car seat just for my son.

My boy was lucky to have so many people who loved him so well.

Back at my shop, I still had to unload the plow that Ace had insisted I take home the previous day. It was a lovely piece and would make a great focus point for someone's garden, but I felt uneasy about having this or any of the other things he'd given me since he might be a murderer after all.

Still, I figured if he was a killer, it was probably better that I not insult him by returning his things, and so I decided to display the plow out in front of the store with a collection of mums that I'd just bought to decorate with. I added in a few decorative gourds and pumpkins, and soon I had a veritable autumn theme going on.

Inside, I didn't have much left to do but be sure everything was priced, twiddle with the displays, and make up my signage about how people could bring in salvage from their property. I decided all that could wait though. I really needed to get out my bonus newsletter so I could get folks their twenty percent coupon for opening weekend.

I needed something more for the letter, though, so I researched "round barns" as I learned even the eight-sided one like ours was called "round" and wrote up a little article. Apparently, Octonia's Round Barn had been one of just over four hundred in the U.S. I was very glad that we'd preserved the poles and beams, and I was even more thrilled that someone was going to turn them into a house.

With my article written, my coupon image made, and the email scheduled for prime email time of one p.m., I felt like I was in good shape for the day and decided to take Mika lunch before picking up Sawyer at the site near home. Saul had texted with the address and said they were having a grand time riding in the forklift so to take my time. I decided to honor that request and grabbed some veggie subs from the local deli in the gas station for Mika and Mrs. Stephenson.

When I got to her shop, Mika pulled out some flavored seltzer from her fridge, and Mrs. Stephenson produced a stash of cheese crackers from her own bag. Now, they had a great meal, and while they ate, we spent the next half-hour talking about nothing important except the best weight of yarn to use for mittens if they were going to get wet. Apparently, I learned, heavyweight wool was the only way to go.

As they finished up their food, I headed out to my car to ride out and get Sawyer, but before I could get my door open, a large hand slammed against the top of it and kept me from opening it. I spun around and stared right into the face of a very large, very angry young man. His pale skin was red with what I could only assume was anger given the glare in his eyes, and he seemed quite determined to stay in this position with me pinned against my car.

Fortunately, I had my keys in my hand, so I was able to force my arm up into his face. "Back up or I'll drive this into your eye."

Apparently, the threat was enough because he backed up and let me step to the side. He didn't move far, though, and while I was tempted to dash back into Mika's store, I expected his long arms would grab me before I got two feet. Instead, I shoved my hand into my back pocket and pressed down one of the volume buttons and the power button on my phone and hoped this feature I'd read about to dial 911 worked.

"You killed him," the man growled as I tried to inch a bit further toward the back of my car.

The last thing I wanted to do was engage in a conversation with a guy this angry, but I didn't have much choice since ignoring him was, I was certain, only going to enrage him further. "Killed who? I don't know what you're talking about."

"My father. I don't know what you did, but I know you killed him." The man stepped a bit closer to me again.

Sometimes, sympathy in the face of anger took people off

their guard, so I tried it. "I'm so sorry to hear about your father's death. I lost my mom. It's terrible."

My tactic did not have the desired effect because he took a long step toward me and pinned me against my car again, this time with one arm on each side of my head. "Do *not* compare me to you, Paisley Sutton."

Well, at least I was clear that he was threatening the person he wanted to threaten. "Please give me some space." I started to raise my keys again, but he pushed my arm down to my side.

"I am not giving you anything. You are a murderer, and you will pay." His grip on my arm tightened.

"Okay then," I whispered. "Then call the police. Tell them what you know. Let them investigate."

The man spat a laugh right into my face. "Are you kidding? Do you think I'm stupid? You're dating the sheriff. How in the world could I expect they'd actually investigate?" He leaned closer to me.

But then, he was gone, and when my eyes refocused, I saw him pinned to the ground beneath Savannah and Santiago. Apparently, my call had gone through. I slumped against my car and watched Savannah slide cuffs around the man's wrists.

As soon as he was secure, with Savannah keeping a firm grip on his shoulder as he sat on the curb, Santiago came over and put my face between his hands. "Are you okay?"

I nodded. "I think so. Who is that?"

"Melvin Smith."

I stared at Santi for a minute. "Another one?"

Santiago smiled. "The grandson. Yes."

"Seriously, people need to buy a baby name book." I tried to laugh, but my chest was still tight with fear. "I think I need to sit down."

He opened my car door, and I slid into the back seat, too overwhelmed to even notice, much, the stash of raisins behind Sawyer's car seat.

"Stay put," Santiago said. "I'm getting Mika." He jogged off in the direction of the shop, and I managed to pull my phone out of my pocket and see that it had, indeed, dialed 911. In fact, the dispatcher was still on the line, softly calling my name.

I put the phone to my ear. "Santiago and Savannah made it," I said. "Thank you."

The woman on the other end let out a long breath. "Good. See you soon, Paisley." I hung up and made a mental note to take her some flowers . . . and learn her name.

Then, I called Saul, briefly explained what had happened, and asked if he could bring Sawyer to me. "Will do," he said, "after we get burgers, if that's okay. He's been talking about *hamboogers* all morning."

"Thanks, Saul. See you in a bit." I let the phone drop beside me on the floor and then leaned my head against the back seat. Now that my brain was clearing, I had a minute to think. Clearly this Melvin Smith thought I had killed his father, and I guess since the man had been at my house just before his death, it wasn't such a big leap.

Maybe the grandson didn't know about Leo Farrow or his grandfather's involvement. Or maybe someone had pointed a finger at me, although I couldn't think of who. Even if Homer or Ace had poisoned Smith, I didn't see either of them as someone to pass the blame to me.

I didn't have much time to think it all through though because just then Mika and Mrs. Stephenson rushed over, and I was soon bustled back into the store, covered with a warm blanket, and handed a cup of hot tea.

"Your dad and Lucille are on their way," Mika said. "I hear there are vanilla scones coming, too."

I laughed. There was not an emergency that Lucille didn't have a baked good for.

As Santiago and Savannah took Smith to the station, I tried to gather myself. Sawyer didn't need to see me being all shaky and sweaty, so I closed my eyes, held my tea with both hands, and took some deep breaths.

The next thing I knew, a tiny body was climbing into my lap and nestling his head under my chin. "Mommy, we can just snuggle?" Saw asked.

I had apparently fallen asleep, and I was pretty sure that there was no better way to wake up than to the person I loved most in the world giving me comfort. I wrapped my arms around him and said, "Thank you, Saw. Let's snuggle."

As I peered over his head, I could see my friends and family gathered together at the table in the back of the store, but when Santiago glanced my way, he smiled and nodded. Clearly, they were okay without me for a few minutes.

Sadly, Saw's snuggling portion of the day was over quickly, and soon, he was up and charging through the store after Mika, who had created a new form of freeze tag involving purple yarn and my father. The three of them were zooming around as Santiago, Savannah, Lucille, Saul, and I sat at the table.

"I need to get your statement, Pais," Santiago said as he squeezed my hand. "Are you up to giving it now?"

I nodded and told them exactly what had happened at my car. He and Savannah took notes, and when I was finished, she said, "Excellent. That's enough for an assault charge if you want to press charges."

It wasn't that I didn't want to press charges, but I didn't know if I had the energy to do that. Between the shop opening, Sawyer, and this whole murder situation, I was already feeling pretty overwhelmed. I looked at Santiago, "Do you need me to press charges?"

Santiago studied my face. "It's really up to you, but in terms of the investigations or your safety, we don't need Smith in jail, if that's what you're asking. I can't be certain, of course, but I think his attack on you was driven by grief and very focused. I don't think he'll hurt you or anyone else again."

Lucille put her hand on my arm. "You need to do what you think is best here, Paisley."

I sighed. "I don't want to press charges, but can you communicate to Smith one condition for me?"

"I'll pass along any message you want," Santiago said, "just know I can't make him comply."

"Understood. Please ask him if he'll bring his grandfather to my shop tomorrow morning to talk with all of us." I didn't exactly know what I was planning to ask either man, but it felt like the least we could make out of this situation was a chance to solve two murders.

Santiago tilted his head and looked at me. "Okay. But Savannah and I will both be there."

"I wouldn't have it any other way," I said. "Lucille, will you see if Dad can convince Homer and Ace to come back, too?"

A hand on my shoulder preceded my father's voice. "I don't think that will be a problem. And Stephen Davis's niece, too, if that's okay. I talked with her this morning."

Santiago looked up at Dad and nodded. "Thanks for convincing her to come in."

I looked between the two men. "Did she know anything?"

"Not much," Savannah said, "but she was going to ask around in her family. She seemed really open to helping."

I picked up my now-cool tea mug and took a sip. "Well, looks like we're going to have quite a gathering in the morning."

SAWYER and I spent the rest of the afternoon at home, playing, watching videos of small children tumbling over, and simply hanging out. I answered a few emails in response to my grand opening email, and by the time we'd had dinner, and Saw was asleep, I had some serious interest in several of my items in the shop because of photos I'd included in the email. It looked like the grand opening was going to be a fun weekend . . . but first I had to get there.

While I stitched the fur lining on Father Winter's cloak and caught up on *Ted Lasso*, I thought a bit about our gathering in the morning. I wasn't quite sure what had prompted me to want to talk to either of the living Melvin Smiths. The first two I'd met hadn't been exactly pleasant people, but I knew there was something we needed to know – something we were missing.

Plus, I'd learned in my years of reporting and research that sometimes stories come forth when people can bounce memories off of each other. Someone remembers one detail which reminds someone else of another. Soon, everyone is remembering more and sharing stories . . . and usually laughter. I didn't know if we'd get to laughter in the morning, but I hoped we'd get to the stories.

I slept fitfully that night, and my dreams all spiraled around a deep, dark hole, shards of glass, and a long, rusty knife. When my alarm went off, I was almost grateful to wake up. Almost.

Sawyer, however, barely moved as I slid out of bed and headed downstairs. Apparently, he needed to catch up on some sleep from his week in the woods with his dad, and I was grateful for a little quiet time to get my head on straight.

Beauregard, however, had other ideas about quiet and began meowing with the gusto of a tiger as soon as he heard my feet on the stairs. I came into the living room to find him talking away to me from his fully reclined position on the couch. Clearly, whatever he needed wasn't urgent enough for him to give up his comfort.

So I made my coffee before I filled his bowl. I could sense his dirty look from behind my back as I stirred in my creamer, but I didn't care. Today, I was going to need to stand up for myself in lots of ways, I expected, and so I practiced on my testy Maine Coon.

. . .

WITH SAWYER finally dressed in his Avengers shirt and his grubbiest jeans so that he could help the members of Saul's crew "organize" the work lot, we loaded up, cat and all, and headed toward my shop. I always loved stores that had animals in them – bookstores with dogs or cats, the hardware store I'd seen once in LA with a resident bunny – so I was determined that Beauregard would become a fixture at my little shop. He didn't like the idea, I don't think, but he didn't like much of anything so I decided to forego his wishes – and ply him with treats, lots of treats.

As soon as we arrived, Sawyer trotted off with a woman who ran one of Saul's crews and Beau settled into the wicker basket that I'd lined with a real sheepskin. He gave me a kind of nasty look but then began to snore, so I figured that was probably as good as I was going to get.

I had brought the coffee carafe from home and was thrilled when Dad and Lucille pulled up with a platter full of Lucille's infamous biscuits and sausage gravy. Dad also took a steaming tray of scrambled eggs out of the back seat, and before I knew it, they had a veritable breakfast bar set up on a folding table just outside the shop.

As I set up folding chairs in a semi-circle, Santiago pulled up with a few more seats. Savannah and I double-checked to be sure we had chairs for everyone we expected, and when we felt sure we were ready, we all sat down with a huff. We had about ten minutes before everyone was due to arrive, according to Saul, who had already helped himself to some biscuits and gravy, and we needed to strategize a bit.

"So this was your plan, Pais. What are you thinking?" Dad asked.

I sighed. "I'm honestly just hoping that someone will share the truth and that we can corroborate what they say based on the others' reaction." As I said my strategy, I realized it was a little lame from a police investigation point of view. It definitely wasn't something that would hold up in court, but my hope was that once the truth was out, people would find they didn't have the energy to protect it anymore.

I'd seen that happen more than once in my research. Someone finally tells a great family secret, and suddenly, it doesn't seem like such a big deal anymore. In this case, of course, murder was a very big deal, but maybe, just maybe, the men who were coming would feel that once it was out, it just needed to be out all the way. I could hope.

Santiago nodded. "I think it could work, Paisley. I do. But you do know that we'll then have to get formal statements."

"Will we?" Savannah asked as she pulled a slim tape recorder from her pocket. "I was thinking. What if Paisley asked for permission to record? She could tell them up front that she may use what they say in future articles for her newsletter, and we could circle the group on record and introduce ourselves, that way it would be clear we are police officers."

Lucille laughed. "The uniforms won't give that away?"

"Not on a recording," Savannah said with a wink. "It's not foolproof, and a judge could throw it out, but maybe . . ."

"Do you think they'll still talk if they're being recorded?" Santiago asked.

I nodded. "My experience is that people often forget they're being recorded if we don't make a big deal about it. Maybe just start the recorder and put it in your cup holder, Savannah?"

"Sounds good," she said.

"It's worth a shot," Dad added, sounding more than a little nervous himself. "Anything you need me to do?"

Santiago looked at me. "Pais?"

"Actually, I'm hoping you'll kick off the conversation, Dad, tell them what you remember, maybe suggest that you aren't sure you're remembering things correctly?"

Dad smiled. "That's easy since that's the truth. I'm not sure how to make heads or tails of any of this." He looked over my head toward the gate. "Show's on."

I turned and saw Homer and Ace walking in with Melvin Smith and an older man with exactly the same ears as his grandson. Beyond them in a pickup by the road, I saw a woman watching us, and when she stepped out, Savannah leaned forward and said, "California Davis-Baca, Stephen Davis's niece."

I smiled. Everyone had come, which was something, and not a small something either. I realized they could either be here to be sure they weren't implicated or simply to throw blame somewhere else, but at least everyone was in the same place to talk about the same thing, finally.

Lucille stepped right into her favorite role as host and invited everyone to the table for food. Once plates and mugs were full, I told everyone that I was glad they were here, mentioned that unless anyone objected, Savannah would be recording our conversation, and then asked everyone to introduce themselves. Most of us knew each other, so this felt a little silly. But fortunately, California Davis-Baca was from out of town, so it didn't seem so weird.

Introductions done and recorded, I again thanked everyone for coming and took the liberty of suggesting that everyone had been invited to help out my dad. "You know my dad is my hero, so it means a lot to me that you're all here," I said.

Dad didn't miss a beat and said, "I know I was there that morning. But I really don't know what I remember anymore. The barn. A rolled up rug. But that's about all I've got. I'm hoping you can help me fill in the rest of the story."

A silence filled the space around us, and, for a brief moment, I wondered if everyone was simply going to keep their mouths shut. But then California said, "I think my uncle may have killed Leo Farrow." The corners of her mouth were turned down in a deep frown, and it looked like maybe she was trying to hold back tears.

Ace studied her face a moment and said, "No, he didn't." He looked at Homer but didn't say anything further.

Melvin Smith, the younger, looked at Ace and then at Homer and then over at his grandfather. The older Melvin stared at his hands but then quietly said, "I did it."

Santiago's eyes shot over to the man and then to Ace before landing on Homer, who was gazing into the middle distance behind Dad's head. "Gentlemen, someone isn't telling the truth here," Santi said. "Ace, care to say anything?"

I admired Santiago's efforts to let the men speak for themselves, but I could feel my anxiety rising. Something was going on here, and I was determined to figure it out. "Please, tell the truth."

Homer's gaze landed on my face. "My father killed Leo Farrow," he said firmly. "He did it."

Ace's shoulders tensed, but then he said, "No, that's not true either. I killed him. I stabbed him."

I threw my hands up in the air and shouted, "So what? Did you all take turns stabbing the man? What is going on here?"

Santiago put a hand on my arm. "They're protecting each other, Paisley. They know I can't make an arrest if I don't have a clear perpetrator, so they're covering up the truth."

None of the men would meet my eyes, and I felt the weight of what Santi had said sink in. "Is that true? Don't you want justice for Farrow? Don't you feel guilty?" The anger was clawing at the inside of my rib cage, and I wanted to shake these men.

California looked at me and said, "I'm sorry, Paisley. Men, please, don't you think Mrs. Farrow and her children deserve the truth after all this time?" Her voice was soft and pleading. "This is all so messed up."

Santiago nodded, "But given that we had a clear suspect,"

he looked at Ace Watkins, "until a few minutes ago, I wanted to wait to talk to the family until I had made an arrest." He sighed. "Now, though, I guess I'm going to have to talk to them."

A fleeting glanced passed from Ace to Homer to Melvin Smith, but no one said a thing.

After a few more moments of tense silence, Dad spoke up. "Will you all tell the truth about this? Did the four of you take Farrow's body in that rug and dump it in the old privy at the barn? Am I remembering that correctly?"

Again, the men looked at each other and then Melvin Smith said, "Yes, the four of us did that. We know that's a crime. We will gladly take our consequences."

"Exactly." Ace looked at Dad and then at Homer, "And we're sorry you boys had to see that."

I let my head fall back and stared at the light blue sky above me. In four days, I was opening my new store, and I so wanted to do that with this all cleared up, for Santiago's sake and my dad's. But also for mine. I wanted a clear and happy grand opening, but that was seeming less and less likely.

10

Everyone left Saul's lot soon after it became clear that we had made as much headway, which was exactly no headway at all, as we could for the day. Rather than clarifying things, this conversation had just made everything more murky.

As I watched Saul make his way over to where his crew was entertaining Sawyer with what looked like a combination of a massive robot battle with the equipment and a mud bog, I tried to take some deep breaths and let all this go. I couldn't control this situation, and I couldn't make people do the right thing. I had to focus on what I could do, and here in this place, I had my boy and my new store . . . I would put my energy there.

Santiago slipped up behind me and slid his arm around my waist. "Can you let this go, Pais? Let Savannah and me handle it?"

I spun toward him and put my forehead against his. "I was just deciding to do that very thing. I so want to help, because I want justice for Farrow and now his family, but also because it was my work that brought all this to light." I took another long, slow breath. "But I have too much to do as it is. This is me letting it go." I stood back, let out a long sigh, and shook out my arms and legs.

"Good for you," Santiago said. "Now, I have a bit of time. What can I help you with here?"

Lucille and Dad came over, and I saw that they had packed up all the food and tidied the front of the store. "Right, you have a crew, so let's get to work. What do you need?" Dad said.

I smiled. "Okay. Well, I have this banner to hang on the fence outside. Can you guys manage that?"

Lucille took it from my hands. "Will I find the twine at the register?"

I nodded, and she and dad took off to hang my grand opening sign. I looked at my boyfriend, "Feel like hanging tulle and lights."

"Only if I can help," Savannah said as she grabbed the ladder from the side of my shed. "Where do you want them?"

Soon Santiago and I were on ladders or chairs with strings of light and pale yellow fabric. Sawyer and Dad had a blast writing "Saturday" in cups poked through the chain-link fence, and Lucille took it upon herself to recruit Savannah and weed all the areas around Saul's construction lot.

Saul even joined in with his skid steer and spread mulch from his stockpile in each spot that Lucille and Savannah cleared. More quickly than I imagined possible, the lot began to look like a real business. "All this place needs is a few shrubs and some bright flowers, and it'll look amazing," Santiago said, as if he was reading my mind.

"Do you think we can do that for spring?" I asked.

"For spring? Why wait that long? I'll go by my favorite nursery this afternoon, and I have time, so I'll come back and plant them. Maybe you and Saw can help?" He grinned when he saw the smile on my face.

"Actually, I think we're busy," I joked. "Sorry."

He leaned over and kissed me. "That's okay. I'll get it done."

I put my face in his neck. "You know I'm kidding."

"Even if you weren't, it would be my pleasure to do this for you," he said as he squeezed me and then jumped up the ladder to attach the last strand of Edison bulbs along the lean-to. Then he climbed down, plugged them in, and clapped when they lit up. With the pale yellow tulle behind them, they really glowed, and even in broad daylight, it looked festive and cozy, just as I hoped.

As everyone else kept working, Santiago and I perched on the register counter as he suggested shrubs and flowers for the landscaping party. We settled on a few viburnum and an array of pansies in various shades of yellow to compliment the décor and to last the winter. Saul was completely on board with the idea because he wanted to support me but also liked the idea of dressing up his lot a bit since he was going to be partnering with me to reconstruct old cabins and sell them as projects for his crew.

While Santiago put his order for the nursery together, I took a few minutes to walk away and look at things. It felt impossible that all of this had come together in just a few short months, but I'd finally let myself accept that when I wasn't too proud to take help and let myself dream big, other people took joy in helping. I could see that in my friends' faces as they worked.

"Mama, it looks so good," Sawyer said as he ran over and hugged my legs. "You're going to sell *everything*."

I hugged my boy close and said, "I hope so, Saw. I hope so." I looked around and decided it was time to get weeding myself. If we were going to do this, we were going to do it right. Sawyer joined in, and since everything green in Saul's lot was a weed, he could go mad pulling up anything he wanted.

After about an hour, we had tidied, mulched, and decorated everything I could think of, and I knew that when the plants came in the next day, everything would be wonderful. Perfect, in fact.

It was only when I saw California Davis-Baca pulling in that my good mood faltered. Farrow's body, Smith's death, and all the intensity of the morning's conversation came flooding back when I saw her step out of the car.

I caught Santiago's eye, and he gestured for me to go on over. Like me, he must have figured she'd have come to the shop to talk to me, not him, and I was glad he trusted me to chat with her.

"Hi California," I said. "See a corbel you couldn't live without?"

She chuckled. "Actually, there's so much here that I'd love, but I really just wanted to talk to you. Do you have a minute?"

"Sure." I looked around. "I can grab chairs from my dad's car if you want."

"No, this will only take a minute." She took a folded piece of paper out of her back pocket. "When I was researching a little over at the library, I came across this article from when Farrow died." She handed me the paper, which turned out to be a printout of a 1942 article from our local *Octonia Eagle*.

"Farrow's wife suspected in husband's disappearance" the headline read. As I read on, I saw that Mrs. Farrow, Eleanor, had been the first and immediate suspect in her husband's death, but according to the article, "an unnamed source informed police that Mrs. Farrow was providing a meal to her pastor's family at the time of her husband's death."

I looked at California. "Interesting," I said. "Why did you want me to see it?"

She shook her head. "I'm not actually sure. Just feels like the men earlier weren't really saying everything."

I took a deep breath. "I know what you mean. But maybe they're just covering for one another," I said.

"Definitely a possibility," she said. "But I wanted you to

know about this just in case." She looked over my shoulder. "Maybe let the sheriff know."

I smiled. "Definitely. Thanks." I looked at her again. "This must be hard, thinking your uncle might be involved."

She tilted her head and nodded. "Yes and no. Uncle Steve wasn't always the nicest guy. Not bad, you know, but kind of mean-spirited, teasing me until I cried. That kind of thing. Sometimes, it feels like I was the only one who could see that, so it's kind of validating to think maybe there was more to it than me just being sensitive."

I sighed. "I know just what you mean. I've been told the same thing from time to time. Now, though, I just think it takes a strong woman to let her emotions show." I held her forearm for a minute and then said, "Thanks so much for this."

She smiled. "You'll keep me posted?"

"On everything," I replied.

As she drove off, I watched her go. Part of me wanted to be suspicious, to think she brought this article to throw aspersions away from her uncle, but what she said about his teasing and her being called sensitive rang too true. I thought she was telling me the truth.

Santiago definitely took interest in the article, and when he showed Savannah, she said, "I guess I'll head back and dig through the files. Thanks, Pais," she said. "Mind if I keep this?"

"Nope. Not at all. California said it came from the *Octonia Eagle*. Maybe worth looking around in there some more?"

"Are you volunteering?" Santiago said.

I laughed. "I wasn't, but I could. One sec." Lucille and Sawyer were frantically weeding the last section of fence in a race to see who could pull up the final weed, and when I walked over, Sawyer took the title, and not because his grand-mother let him win either. He out and out won.

As he hauled a pile of weeds over to the woods at the edge of the lot, I asked Lucille if she minded taking him home with her for a bit. "I've got a bit of research to do." I told her about his plan to landscape the lot later in the afternoon, and she grinned.

"You'd better keep him," she said.

I blushed. "I intend to," I whispered and looked across the lot to where he was on the phone. He was so handsome, and so kind, too. I felt very fortunate to have him in my life.

With Lucille's full blessing, Sawyer jumped into her car, strapped himself into his car seat, and gave me a wave as his Baba drove him across the lot to where his Boppy was talking to Saul. I could hear his favorite song, "Party Freeze Dance" playing through the open windows. The child was in heaven.

Before Santiago dropped me off at the library on his way into town, we made plans for meeting back at the shop. "I'll be over after I pick up the plants, probably about three."

"Perfect," I said and kissed his cheek as I opened the car door. "This shouldn't take long. See you then."

Inside the library, the smell of books made me smile, and I headed straight to the local research room at the back. I'd once spent most of a semester doing research on our high school basketball team in this room when I was in eighth grade. Our history teacher, Mrs. Cagle, had wanted us to get good with archival resources, and so she'd assigned groups of us research in various areas. It took us a while to figure out that basketball was often called "caging" in the early twentieth century, but once we knew that, we were on the move. And I loved spinning through the microfilm and hunting down tiny articles and huge spreads about the local team and athletes.

I could feel that same excitement as I sat down at the machine now. I knew from that experience – thank you, Mrs. Cagle – that I had to look a bit more broadly than just at the dates in question. Articles could come out weeks or even months after an event, so I started with a week before Farrow's death, just in case there was something relevant there.

Sure enough, two days before he died on November 14, 1945 he was arrested for being drunk and disorderly in town. There wasn't much detail in the news blotter article about the arrest, but apparently, he'd been on Main Street spouting off about how he had to stay home and keep things in order instead of fighting a war that wasn't his.

That all lined up with what Dad had said about Farrow's thoughts on the war, but Dad hadn't told me the man was belligerent. Of course, this could have been a one-time incident, but I doubted it. If you lost control enough to lose it in public once, I expected it was probably a frequent happening.

After printing out that article, I kept digging. The next article I located was the one about Farrow's death that California had given me. I printed out a copy for myself and then kept on looking. A couple days later, the paper reported that no suspects had been named in his disappearance, and then finally, two weeks later, a very brief article said that it was presumed he had run away to dodge the draft and that donations of food were being taken by Mrs. Farrow at her residence.

I was glad that our paper had been focused on the lives and experiences of people back in those days, but I couldn't help wishing there was a GoFundMe page or something for Mrs. Farrow. I might have gotten more updates on things through there. As it was, the story of his death seemed to track with everything we had known before.

With a half hour more before I needed to go pick up Sawyer, I spun through a few more days of papers and was about to shut off the machine and put away the microfilm when a headline caught my eye. "Missing Man's Oldest Son Enlists," it read.

I scrolled through the article and saw that, sure enough, Luke Farrow, Leo's son, had enlisted in the army just three weeks after his father had disappeared, supposedly for dodging the draft. The article went on to quote Luke and say that he was only doing his duty like so many men before him had done. The report also suggested that Luke Farrow was too young to join up "having only finished eighth grade last year," but no further details or quotes were given.

I couldn't help but wonder how Mrs. Farrow felt to think her husband had run away to avoid doing what her son volunteered to do. Was she proud? If so, of whom?

I scanned the film a bit further just in case, but when I didn't see anything for two more weeks, I packed up and headed out to get Sawyer from his grandparents. When I arrived, he was in their huge, inflatable pool with a giant octopus floaty thing. And he looked giddy.

"Look, Mama, I splash you," he said with such a smile of delight that I couldn't even bring myself to jump out of the way. Soon enough, I was soaked, and when I made a goofy face and leaped in the pool with him, Saw squealed with delight.

We had a great time, but we all had to get back to the shop to do the landscaping. Sawyer was exhausted but content, and I felt much the same, especially when I saw Santiago's car pull into Saul's driveway. Something about his presence simply soothed me. Even in the midst of all this hard stuff with Farrow's and now Smith's murders and with the excitement and stress of opening my shop, I felt calm because I knew he was beside me. Clearly, this was what love felt like.

In the next few minutes, though, as everyone showed up at my shop to help us plant the surprisingly vast number of shrubs and flowers Santiago had bought, I decided to put out of my mind what I couldn't control. As we worked, I told Santiago about what I'd found at the library, and he and Savannah were going to look into that information. Now, though, I had a business to open, and I was determined to make the grand opening a huge success.

Saul's crew chipped in to help with digging holes, and Santiago and Dad got those into the ground. Mika had gotten Mrs. Stephenson to cover the shop, and so she and I planted the pansies and also a large array of mums Santiago had picked up. Within a couple of hours, the entire place looked like a fall cavalcade of color. It was going to be some work to keep all these watered if the heat kept up and the rain held off, but for the transformation Saul's lot had gone through, that bit of extra work would be worth it for all of us.

With the plants in, the on-site advertising up, and the wares all set, I now had a few minutes to concentrate on setting up on my online ads. I had made a Facebook page, and I was on Instagram, but now, I needed to do the real push. So Sawyer and I headed over to Mika's shop so that he could play, and I could work for another half hour.

Before she left, Mrs. Stephenson had set out a special yarn craft that involved construction paper, glue, and short strips of yarn, and Sawyer was intent on whatever he was making. From a distance, it looked like it could either be a dragon or a volcano. It was hard to tell.

As I scheduled my posts and got my images ready, I tried to focus on what I was excited about with the shop – the chance to give old things a new home, to save some gems of history from the landfill, to grow my business as a single mother. I'd long ago learned that stories were what connected people to something, so I tried to write posts and share images with people and places behind them. In some ways, this was my favorite part of the work.

I was just scheduling a photo of the plow that Ace Watkins had sold me when my mind made one of those lateral leaps that happen when we're only letting things spin through our subconscious. I got to thinking about the way a plow carves furrows in a field, then about my own garden, where every few feet I unearth a piece of pottery. I wondered what, if anything, we might find if we turned over some of the ground around where the barn had stood. I knew it was a long shot, especially since we'd combed the ground so thoroughly when we took the building down. But maybe there'd be something.

I texted Santiago and asked if he thought it worthwhile, and he laughed. "I just drove out there with my metal detector. Want to come? We still have a couple hours of light."

"Are you serious?" I said with a laugh of my own. "Yeah, I want to come. Sawyer and I will be there in twenty minutes. Just need to finish up something."

As I posted my last images and helped Sawyer clean up the extensive mess he'd made, I pondered how it was that Santiago had managed to have the same idea at the same time. Something about observing clues and similar experiences around the same time. But part of me wondered. Maybe this was what having a true connection to someone felt like.

Either way, I was glad we were on the same page, and fortunately, Sawyer was super excited to use a metal detector – or met-tector as he called it, so he wasn't even resistant to the change in plans. In fact, for the entire ride there, he kept talking about how he was going to find pirate treasure. I couldn't help but hope he was right both literally and metaphorically, and when I told him I hoped so, he said, "And if we find some, Mama, I will share it with you."

"Thank you, Sawyer. That's very kind of you." Sometimes, it felt like maybe this parenting thing was going right.

As soon as we pulled up to the field where the barn had been, I unbuckled Saw, and he was off like a shot to where Santiago stood with detector and headphones. I made my way over just in time to hear Santi say, "These are for you. You help me listen for beeps, okay?"

I leaned over and kissed Santiago's cheek and then wandered the field while the boys in their headphones let the machine do the work. I wasn't very confident that I'd find anything by just looking. I wasn't really that confident that the metal detector would find anything or that there was anything to find at all, but I figured it couldn't hurt to look and get in some steps anyway.

The pasture ran up to the edge of the woods where the slope of the mountain got steeper, and given that this setting with pastures and wood-lined mountains was one of my absolutely favorites, I decided to head that way and see what history I might find in the wild edges. There was just something special about finding a tree with barbed wire embedded in it, a testimony to the fact that it had once marked a pasture or farmyard. When I found those things or abandoned equipment in a field, I always felt like I had done a little time traveling. It was one of the best parts of my job.

As I approached the edge of the forest, I saw an old fence line, the posts almost rotted off from the ground, and decided to follow it. It went in a straight line to the forest just east of where the barn had stood, and I could almost picture cattle wandering into the tree line for shade on a hot summer day.

I made my way along the barbed wire and into the woods a few feet. From there, I could look back along the small valley toward the barn site and then on to the hollow rising up into the mountains to the west. Small houses dotted the hillside, and while I knew the people who lived up that way weren't wealthy financially, I couldn't help but think they had some real riches in that view.

My eyes traveled over each house, but when I got to a small, low house just up the hill from where I stood, my gaze stopped. There, someone was standing with binoculars looking down the hill, right at Santiago and Sawyer. I couldn't tell who it was, but they were definitely watching the boys. Something about that sent a chill up my spine, and I wanted to sprint to my little boy. But I knew it wouldn't be good to give any indication to that person that I'd seen them looking down. So I continued to follow the fence line through the woods and then out a few feet further west and closer to that house.

I acted like I was just looking around, but I kept flicking my attention toward the house and could see that the person was watching me sometimes and the boys sometimes. Clearly, they were interested in what we were doing. I needed to let Santiago know that, so I quickened my pace just a little and made my way back to where the guys were searching.

"Anything?" I asked with a smile and full awareness that I was being watched.

Santiago shook his head. "A lot of bottle caps, which Sawyer loves, but nothing for us. You see anything?"

I shook my head very deliberately even as I said, "Just someone from a couple houses up watching us with binoculars."

Santiago studied my face and kept his attention fixed on me. "Do they know you saw them?"

"I don't think so," I said. "But that's weird, right?"

"Which house was it?" Santiago asked as Sawyer leaned his head against my thigh and let me play with his hair.

"Two up, I think. Gray boards, metal roof, red pickup in the driveway," I said.

Santiago took a slow, deep breath. "That's Leo Farrow's place."

11

We searched a bit more around the barn site, mostly for the sake of appearances and then loaded up in the car. We had covered a lot of ground in just over an hour. I suggested we drive up that way, see if we could catch a glimpse of the person who was watching us, but Santiago wisely pointed out that it might seem suspicious that we drove up the mountain at this point.

"I'll go up later in a patrol car. One of us drives through once a week or so anyway just to check on things, talk with folks who are out and about. It'll seem natural," he said.

"Or better yet, maybe Savannah should do it since you were just here," I suggested.

"Good idea," he said. "We definitely have to figure out what that was about."

"What are you talking about?" Sawyer asked from the backseat.

"Nothing, Love Bug. Just we saw someone with binoculars."

"Were they doing some bird watching?" he asked.

I laughed. "Maybe, bud. They were looking around for

sure." I turned to look at him. "Want to do some bird watching with your binoculars when we get home?"

"Yeah, and you get your 'noculars,' too, Mama." He smiled at me and then sat back to look out the window. My dad had given Sawyer a pair of binoculars, but when a friend gifted him an entire insect hunting set with binoculars, the old ones became mine and the fancy new ones his. It worked. We spent a few concentrated minutes on the porch looking for birds.

Or I should say I pretended to watch for birds most of the time, pointed out the occasional bird that crossed my path for Saw, and spent most of the time thinking about who from Farrow's house would be watching us and checking my phone to see if Santi had texted.

Finally, at almost eight, after Sawyer and I had exhausted bird watching, playing on his playground, and looking for worms in the garden, Santi called. "I expect you've been hoping to hear from me," he said with a chuckle.

I felt the heat rise to my cheeks. "You know me too well," I said as I pulled weeds from around the pepper plants and watched Sawyer "aerate" the soil in what would be our garlic bed.

"Savannah took a ride up and talked to a bunch of the neighbors, told them we were looking into Farrow's murder again. She didn't get any new information." He paused for what I knew was a dramatic effect.

I waited a millisecond and then blurted, "Okay, but what did she find out at the Farrow place?"

Santiago chuckled. "You are such an information hound, Ms. Sutton. She spoke with one Luke Farrow."

I stood up and stared across the yard. "What?! The Luke Farrow who enlisted. How is that possible? He would have to be in his nineties."

"Ninety-one to be exact. Once Savannah got him talking,

apparently, he had a lot to say, but not much about his dad's death." Santiago sighed.

"Oh, that's disappointing." I felt the surge of energy that I'd just gotten slip away at his words. "So another dead end?"

At that moment, car tires sounded on the gravel driveway, and Sawyer climbed over the fence to Santiago's approaching sedan. "Surprise. I just had to see your face when I tell you this next part," he said into the phone.

I stared at him as I held the phone to my ear and slowly walked his way.

"You can hang up now, Paisley," he laughed.

"Oh, right," I said as I pushed the button on my phone and slipped it into my pocket.

"You are adorable," he said as he met me in the yard by the garden. "Is there anything you're not curious about?"

I stared up at the sky for a minute. "Hockey," I said.

"Fair enough," he said with a smile. "Okay, so Savannah wasn't sure Luke Farrow was telling the truth, but then, she didn't want to raise too much suspicion or make him cautious. So she left."

I stared at Santiago for a minute. "You wanted to see my face while you told me *that*?"

"Oh no, it's this next part I wanted to witness." He pulled me into a hug and looked down at my face. "As soon as Savannah was out of sight of the house, a man about my age stepped out of the trees down the road a bit and flagged her down."

I pulled back. "Wow. That sounds a little creepy."

"Yeah, but get this? It was Landon Farrow."

I held his gaze and waited.

"Leo's great-grandson." He watched my expression as it went from apathy to shock.

"Whoa." I pulled back from him and looked over the garden to think. "Great-grandson? Where's the grandson?"

"He died a few years back. Cancer," Santiago said quietly. "Apparently, Landon goes up every few days to check on his grandparents. Be sure they have what they need."

"Wait?! Luke Farrow's wife is still alive, too?"

"Sure is. Annie is a spry eighty-seven, according to Savannah."

"Wow, so what did Landon want to tell Savannah?" I asked.

"He said that he didn't think his grandfather knew anything, but he might. Asked us, though, to not come up there again because he didn't want to upset his grandfather."

"That's interesting, I guess." I felt a shiver run down my spine, but nothing in my mind gave me a real clue about why that was.

Santiago pulled me close. "Maybe we can grow old together like Luke and Annie." He almost whispered the words, but he didn't look away.

My heart kicked, and I smiled. "I'd like that," I said. It was a tender moment that was interrupted when Sawyer blew the horn on Santiago's car and then grinned like the Joker.

"Stop talking," my son said. "Let's eat." He launched himself out of the car window and ran toward the house. "I'll make noodles."

Santiago and I exchanged a glance and then jogged after him to be sure we were there when he began his cooking preparations.

WE WALKED in just as Saw was reaching for a box of noodles.Did you wash your hands, Saw?" I asked.

He held up his grubby mitts. "They're clean," he said.

I rolled my eyes. "Seriously?" I said as I took his dirt-encrusted fingers in mine. "This is what you consider clean."

"I'm just kidding. I'm playing a trick on you." Then he

trotted off to the bathroom to wash his hands while Santiago and I did the same in the kitchen.

Sawyer did a surprisingly good job of cooking his macaroni and cheese noodles, and when I took his chicken nuggets out of the oven, he said, "This is my favorite dinner, Mama."

I smiled. "I'm glad, Saw."

Soon, we were all eating – Santiago and I had a chicken Caesar salad I whipped up – and laughing at more of Sawyer's made-up jokes that had absolutely no sense behind them. We finished dinner and the cleaning up, and then Santiago and Sawyer took the metal detector out into our yard to see what they could find while I sat under the porch light and sewed for a bit.

The guys didn't find anything but fairly recent nails and some old barbed wire on their hunt, but Santiago offered to leave the detector with us so that Sawyer and I could do more detecting the next day when there was better light. Saw was giddy, and I was pretty excited, too. We had some old outbuildings and what I thought was an old privy hole behind the house, and I was eager to see what we might find. I just hoped it wasn't another skeleton.

THE NEXT MORNING, Sawyer was out of bed at dawn and ready to head out with the detector. I waylaid a tromp through the dewy grass with some waffles with Nutella and a requirement that Saw have on both shoes and socks. It was still pretty damp when we went out, but there is nothing that will stop a determined three-year-old for long, I'd found.

We spent the next two hours on the ground in the dirt with the metal detector under the chicken coop and the old kitchen, and it was incredibly fun for both of us. Sawyer found some old canning jar lids, and I managed to locate an old saw blade that was in pretty good shape and would make a great wall-hanging for me to sell in the shop.

After a quick shower for me and a washcloth bath for Sawyer, we headed in to see Mika. I felt like I had a million things to do for the store, but my brain was firing too fast for me to focus. A rambunctious little man wasn't helping, so I figured I might as well surrender to the situation and let the wildness ensue.

We rode with the windows down and Bob Dylan's "Along The Watchtower" blaring as Sawyer sang along to some semblance of the lyrics. I laughed, and we danced, and by the time we got to Mika's store, I was more relaxed than I'd been in days.

The store was busy, so Sawyer and I teamed up and helped people find things. I swear Mika made more sales because of Saw's dimples than she usually did. The three of us tended customers and tidied shelves, mostly shelves that Saw untidied first, and by the time she closed up at five, we were all giddy and laughing.

We decided to have dinner at the Mexican place down the road and invited Santiago and Chris to join us. I hadn't heard a lot of details about how things were going with Chris, but I did know they were texting a lot and had made plans for a second date on Saturday after they came to my grand opening reception. It seemed hopeful, especially if they were both willing to double date with us on the spur of the moment.

The guys were already at a table when we arrived, and when four frozen margaritas arrived at the table along with the nachos and salsa, both Mika and I let out a little whoop. It had been a good day, but a good day in retail means a physically taxing day. The tequila in those margaritas was just the relaxation trigger we needed.

And when Sawyer's virgin margarita showed up a moment later in a paper cup with an umbrella and a straw, everyone was very content to drink and chat for a bit. Eventually, though, the conversation did turn back around to Leo Farrow and Melvin Smith's murders. I was dying to know what Landon Farrow had told Santiago and Savannah, but I knew that if Santiago was comfortable sharing what they learned he would.

Fortunately, I didn't have to wait long because as soon as we caught Chris up on what had been happening, Santiago said, "There's new news. Well, maybe not news since when I talked to your dad, Pais, he seemed quite familiar with this fact, but apparently, Leo Farrow was quite the amateur photographer, took pictures of everything about his life."

Mika laughed. "A black and white Instagrammer before his time," she said.

I smiled. "What kind of things did he take pictures of?"

"Really, everything, according to Landon. His chickens, the sunrises and sunsets, interesting leaves. Anything and everything." Santiago paused, and all three of us leaned in. "But he also took pictures around the house, and after we found his body, his great-grandson started looking through the pictures."

"He found something?" Chris said rather loudly before realizing that he was attracting attention.

"He did," Santiago said more quietly. "He found pictures of his great-grandmother holding things like knives or pokers as she stood over Leo."

I sat back. "Whoa, that's creepy. Were they posed or impromptu shots?"

"Hard to tell," Santiago said as he sat back. "It seems weird that someone would grab their camera when they were being threatened, but I've seen more strange things on the job."

"Maybe she didn't like having her picture taken?" Mika said.

Santiago bounced his head back and forth. "Maybe. She looks very angry in the photos, so she was either a very good actress, or she was very, very upset with her husband."

Sawyer took a long slurp from his drink and said, "She was trying to kill him."

I looked at my son, who regularly talked about killing Beauregard in the same breath that he talked about how he'd love him forever, and said, "What do you mean Love?"

"The knife. You can kill someone with a knife. That's why I can't run with them or have them much." He sipped more of his drink.

"Out of the mouths of babes," Santiago said. "He may well be right. If so, then I'll have to look into it, even if I'm not sure it's relevant to our investigation given how many confessions we already have." He sighed heavily.

I was about to suggest we steer the conversation in a new direction because the idea that my three-year-old might have just provided valuable insight on a *murder* investigation was a bit much for me when a woman walked over to my table.

"Hi Summer," I said as I stood up to hug her. "It's good to see you."

She smiled and waved at the table before looking at Sawyer and saying, "You must be Sawyer Sutton."

He hid behind my leg and whispered, "Sawyer Brown Sutton." He always said all three of his names if someone said his last name.

I looked back toward the direction from which she came. "You here alone?"

"Yep. It's something I do from time to time, just to get out in society more. And these guys have the best salsa around." She pointed to the empty bowl in the middle of our table. "I see you all agree."

Everyone smiled, and then Mika said, "Would you like to join us?" It was the polite thing to say, especially since our food hadn't yet arrived, but somehow, the invitation made me a little uneasy. I chalked that up to my crime-solving son, though, and shook off the feeling.

"Yes, please," I said as I moved to get an extra chair from the wall behind us.

"Well, if I wouldn't be intruding, I'd love the company, and to get to know you a bit more, Sawyer." She smiled and slid her chair on the other side of my son. "So what were you all talking about?"

Santiago met my eyes, and I took the hint quickly. "Oh, just the goings on about town. You heard that they're thinking of widening the 29/33 intersection, didn't you?" It was the most banal conversation topic in the world, but it was the first thing I could think of that might let us chat and give Mika and Chris the hint that we had to discontinue our earlier conversation.

"Oh, I hadn't, no," Summer said with a smile as the server brought her a glass of water and some fresh chips and salsa for the table. "Can you just move me over here? Sorry for the trouble."

The server smiled with a look of mild annoyance that seemed too intense as small as the request was given that she only had four tables. Still, she moved Summer's utensils and placemat to her new seat and headed back to get our food.

When Sawyer's quesadilla arrived, he put two fingers on it, declared it gross, and refused to eat. Fortunately, I was old hat at the eating refusal world and decided to simply ignore his comments while also giving him my phone so he could quietly watch videos. Sometimes that worked to help him eat mindlessly. Not the best habit to instill in a child, but the boy had to get some food in him.

Meanwhile, in the conversation about the road widening, all of us were in agreement, it seemed, that it was a good thing, but then, we weren't personally invested in the antique shops and small stores that were being demolished to make room. In fact, despite my love of old buildings, I was going to be glad to see the ill-maintained old structures go. I did hope, though, that I'd get a chance to salvage there, so I kept my mouth shut about that.

The food was delicious, and our conversation slowed while we all ate. I had chicken tacos with mole, and while they weren't the best I'd ever had – that title was reserved for a food truck in a little town called St. Marin's that I'd once visited – they were really good. The spice combined with the sweet of the margarita really hit the spot.

That is until Summer steered our conversation back to Farrow's murder. "Any further information on that body you found under my barn?" she asked.

Santiago played it cool, although I felt his leg tense under the table, and took a bite of his burrito. "Sorry, I'm not allowed to talk about that with civilians," he said as he wiped his mouth.

Summer's brow furrowed. "But I just heard you talking about it a few minutes ago."

I winced. We had made a mistake.

"Sawyer said someone was trying to kill someone." She looked at each of us, and when we stared blankly back at her, she said, "Oh, maybe you were talking about someone else."

Sawyer looked up at me and gave me a puzzled look, but when I shook my head no just enough for him to see it, he looked back at his videos. I breathed a sigh of relief. My son could be shy, but when he got going, sometimes, he didn't stop talking. This was one of those times when his shyness was better.

"It was a show we watched," Mika added. "I was just telling everyone about it." She glanced at Sawyer. "Probably not my wisest move with little ears present."

Go, Mika, I thought. She'd both covered up our conversation and protected Sawyer from more murder discussion in one comment.

I looked over at Summer and said, "Yep, you know *Manifest*? It's this sort of time travel, spiritual, mystery thing."

Summer shook her head. "Nope, don't watch much TV myself. Sounds interesting though." She glanced over at Sawyer. "If you don't mind me asking, did you find anything when you were out in the field yesterday?"

This woman was not going to let this go, and Santiago must have known it. "Nope, nothing. I decided it was worth taking a little bit more in-depth look, but we didn't turn up anything, did we, Saw?"

Sawyer looked up at him and said, "What?"

"Nothing, Buddy," Santi said with a laugh. "Just watch your videos." Then he turned back to Summer. "I hope you don't mind that we went out there. I saw your alpacas in the field, but since they were grazing along the other side, I hoped it wouldn't disturb them for us to be there."

"Oh goodness, no. Totally fine. They're pretty sedate critters, unless they have babies, but the one mama isn't due for a couple more weeks yet." Her voice got more serious then. "If you would, though, call me next time to let me know. It's disconcerting to see someone on your property when you aren't expecting them."

I flicked my eyes over to Santiago, and he was nodding. "Of course. I should have done that yesterday. So sorry. Saw and I were just so excited about metal detecting that I was rude, I apologize." He held Summer's gaze, and when she smiled, I knew she believed him.

I, however, knew that he had intentionally not called her because he didn't need her permission to visit a crime scene.

"How's Dom?" Mika asked as Chris reached over and took her hand.

I smiled, but then I lost track of Mika and Chris when Summer spoke.

"I expect he's fine. I haven't seen him. Just not my type, you know." Her voice was brisk, almost cold.

Chris frowned but didn't say anything, and we finished the rest of our meal in silence with a bit of spattered conversation about stuff going on in Octonia. Clearly, things were more awkward now, and I wished Summer hadn't joined us. But soon enough, we were done, Santiago was paying the bill for all of us, including Summer, and we were out on the sidewalk.

I really wanted a chance to talk with Mika and Chris about Dom, and apparently, Santiago had the same idea because he said, "Nice to see you, Summer." Then, to Chris and Mika, "Ready to go, guys?"

We all turned and followed Santiago to his sedan and climbed in. Santiago started the engine, waiting to see – as Southern politeness dictated – if Summer's car started and she got going. Then he pulled out, swung up the block, and parked behind the library, just steps from where my car was parked near Mika's shop.

When the car was parked, Chis grabbed his phone out of the console and shot off a quick text before saying to all of us, "Dom is going to be surprised and hurt."

A moment later, his phone rang, and Mika, Sawyer, and I stepped out of the car to give the three friends some time to talk. Meanwhile, the three of us strolled up and around the library to the side street by the courthouse. The evening was cooling off, and as twilight set in, the old buildings of the courthouse square looked particularly magical with the orange glow of sunset coming off the bricks.

I decided it wasn't going to do us any good to speculate about the murders or about what Dom was going to say, and I was really wary of having Sawyer hear more about this case. So I pried into something that I was very curious about and could understand more deeply. "So, you and Chris?" I said.

Mika blushed. "Yeah. He's really great."

"And things are going well?" Like I couldn't tell that at dinner or from Mika's reaction here.

"Really well. I like him. A lot. Maybe too much already," she said with a little catch in her voice.

"Stop shaming yourself for what you feel. Just go with it. You're smart and wise, and all this will work out as it should." I was really good at giving this advice, and far less good at taking it. But I still meant what I said.

"Chris is nice," Sawyer chimed in.

Mika smiled. "Thanks. That helps." We walked on a bit more, and then she said, "I've been thinking about Melvin Smith. Someone gave him something in his food or drink, right? Isn't that what Santiago thinks?"

I glanced down at Sawyer, who had stopped to study an ant on the sidewalk. "Yeah, that's their working theory." The ant grew boring, apparently, because Sawyer walked on in a few moments. We turned onto Main Street and looped back toward Santi's car.

"And he thinks that happened at your house?" Mika asked.

"Or just before, I guess," I said. "Why?"

"Well, if it was at your house, then that means someone there really had something to hide and must have thought Melvin Smith knew about it, right?"

I took a deep breath as I thought about what she'd said. I'd been so preoccupied with the idea that he might have been poisoned at my house that I hadn't given much more thought to the fact that, if so, that meant the murderer had been at my house, too. "I suppose so."

We didn't have further time to talk about it as we walked up to the car. The two guys were leaning on the hood waiting. "Dom okay?" Mika asked when we reached them.

"Yeah, a little hurt and angry, maybe, but okay," Chris said.

"It just didn't work out?" I asked as Santiago picked up Sawyer, who had come to rest his head on Santi's leg.

"Apparently, 'it' didn't even get started. He thought they were really connecting that day, but then she blew him off later, hasn't answered his texts, and the one time she did answer when he called, she said she wasn't looking for a relationship and to please leave her alone." Chris was definitely more than a little angry.

"Ouch," Mika said. "I definitely thought she was into him, too. Wonder what that was about?"

"Who knows?" Chris said before slipping an arm around Mika's waist. "You aren't going to start ignoring my texts and calls now are you?" He smiled at her in a way that said he already knew the answer to his question.

"You never know," Mika said with a wink. "I might suddenly get very busy."

"Speaking of busy," I said, "I need to get home and get some sleep. And so does this guy." Sawyer had dozed off on Santiago's shoulder. "See you all Saturday?"

"Saturday? I'm coming to your shop tomorrow to help you get everything set up. Nine a.m. work?" Mika said.

I smiled. "That's perfect. Thanks."

As Santiago walked me to my car and helped me get Sawyer into his seat, I kept thinking about Summer's behavior. Something was definitely up with her. I just didn't know what that something was.

12

The next morning, Sawyer was still sleeping soundly when I got up at five-thirty, my head spinning with all I wanted to accomplish. So I double-checked that my emails and ads were ready to go for the day and spent a few minutes with the manual for the cash register I needed to set up this morning.

But when I heard Saw stirring, I settled myself on the couch with my coffee to take some deep breaths for just a few minutes and center myself.

More and more, I'd been learning that my tendency to jump ahead into the next thing or to keep the list of things I needed to do constantly spinning in my mind made me very anxious. So I was meditating more with an eye toward the moment I was in. I was getting better at the "be here now" mantra, but it was hard.

Still, by the time Sawyer came down, I was feeling much more calm, and I'd felt that twinkle of some understanding about Melvin Smith's murder coming into more sharp focus, too. I expected I'd get some flash of insight later today when I wasn't really thinking about the case at all.

When we got to Saul's lot, Mika was already there with the shop open. I'd given her a key so that I had back-up if something happened and I couldn't get there to open, just like I had keys to her store. Now, she was busy watering the mums by the front door.

"I should hire you," I said as I stepped out of the car. "Thank you."

"Are you kidding? It's always fun to help out in someone else's shop, like cleaning someone else's house, no pressure." She smiled and moved the hose to the next plant. "Remember in college when we babysat for extra money and would clean the parents' houses after the kids were in bed? We really should have charged more."

"We definitely should have. And I'll pay you in donuts, okay?"

Sawyer, who had been literally climbing over the car, said, "Donuts. I want donuts."

"Baba made donuts for us this morning," I said. "They'll be here soon."

"Yay," Sawyer said. "Oh no, Mama. You forscot to have your coffee." His look of alarm was super touching.

"It's okay, Saw. I've got your mama covered," Mika said as she handed me the largest latte available from the local coffee shop. "Vanilla with a dash of cinnamon."

"Perfect," I said as I took a long pull from the cup and watched Mika coil up the hose and put it against the shed.

"Now what?"

"Feel like you can help me set up the register?" I asked.

"I can help," Sawyer said with a grin.

I looked at my son and suppressed my groan at the idea of a three-year-old assisting with the computer-based machine. He spent most of the time when I had to be on my computer near me hitting combinations of buttons that made my laptop do things I didn't know it could do, so the idea that he might throw off my accounting from the get-go sent me into a mild panic.

Fortunately, Saul approached just then and said, "I know your mama probably needs you, Saw, but I was wondering if you wanted to help me drive the big dump truck." Saul looked over at me and winked.

"The big, *big* one?" Sawyer asked.

"Yep, the big, big one." Saul smiled as Sawyer took off across the lot to the huge dump truck idling nearby. "I'll try to keep him busy," Saul said as he jogged after Sawyer.

I breathed a sigh of relief and went around to the back of my car to lift out the register. When I'd first started shopping for these things, I'd thought of the old cash registers at the country stores like in *Little House on the Prairie,* but this thing was really just a cash drawer, a keyboard, and a tablet with a card swiper. So simple and so lightweight.

But I had a reputation, at least with Mika, for being able to flub up any piece of software upon opening it. Once, I had bought a very nice new laptop. When I opened it, I accidentally had my hand on the power key and locked the entire machine up so completely that I had to take it to a helpdesk to get it running. Then there was the time that I'd set up four different accounts for the same year of the same tax software and kept having to redo my taxes with every log-in. She was right to be concerned.

So she took the lead on getting the machine up and running while I triple-checked to be sure all the items in the shop and outside under the lean-to were priced. Then, she walked me through how to ring up sales in "test" mode so that I could make some egregious errors – which I did – but within an hour or so, I had it down pretty well and felt good about running sales through it on Saturday.

With the technical aspects of sales down, we had to set up the inventory system, but fortunately, this kind of thing was my forte. I loved thinking about systems and processes, so I took out the list I'd made of general categories and talked it through with Mika as she began to set up the register in the way my inventory would be tracked.

We created categories for glassware and furniture; boards; doors and windows; and every other general grouping of old stuff we could think of. Mika even suggested we create a group for "Tinies" like spoons and old buttons because I had a few bins of that kind of thing, and since those items were readily available at estate sales and such, I could always add more if they sold well. Finally, we put in her knitwear before adding a Miscellaneous category that would require me to input the exact item so that I could make new, larger groups as I saw what we had missed in our initial set-up.

Further down the line, I'd get barcodes and a scanner, but for now, a manual system worked. And I hoped it would help me plan for sales as I looked at salvage jobs. Just logging the categories had me pretty excited, and I hoped that the sales at the shop would be the kind of income stream that could really supplement the big sales I had for lots like the old barn we'd just taken down.

I was in the process of telling Mika how I'd be tracking those in the inventory system when I heard gravel fly in the parking lot. It sounded like hailstones as rocks hit the metal pieces under the lean-to, and I jogged out the door to see who it was. I stopped short as a tall man with long black hair and a very pale complexion stepped out of the car and marched toward me. I had the momentary impression that I was being stalked by a vampire, but I quickly pulled myself back to reality as he stepped directly in front of me.

This was the second time this week that a man had gotten physically confrontational with me, and I was just stressed enough and just fed up enough to stand up for myself this time.

"Back off, sir," I said as I put my arms out in front of me and pushed his body back.

He tried to step forward again, but I kept my arms out to hold him away. Just then, I felt two big shoulders line up on either side of mine and saw two of Saul's male crew members beside me with the rest of the men and women coming across the yard at a clip.

Saul sprinted over and said, "Can I help you?" to the man who was still actively trying to get closer to me.

"Her, she's stirring up trouble about my great-grandaddy," the man said to Saul before turning to me. "You have no idea what you're doing, Paisley Sutton."

The men beside me gently moved me behind them as Saul stepped in front of all of us. "I don't know what you're talking about," I managed to say before I heard the most painful sound in the world: my son screaming and crying for me.

I turned to see one of Saul's crew members holding Sawyer as he reached and struggled to run to me. I wanted so badly to go to him, to tell him it was all okay, but I wasn't about to lead this man with clear rage issues closer to my son. No way. So I blew Saw a kiss and turned back to confront this guy.

I expected that when I looked back at him I'd see his anger-filled face, but instead, tears were beginning to slip from his eyes. "Is that your son?" he asked.

I tilted my head, glanced at Saul, and then nodded.

"I'm so sorry," he whispered and turned back to his car and drove away.

I stared after him for just a moment before I heard a thunderfall of footsteps coming my way and bent down to scoop Saw up in a tight hug. "I'm okay Love. I know that was scary, but I'm okay," I whispered into his head as he sobbed against me.

"Why was that man yelling, Mama?" Saw stammered as his sobs began to subside.

I looked at Saul and then said to Sawyer, "I don't know Love. I really don't know."

When Santiago arrived a few minutes later, Sawyer was enjoying some videos on my phone while he drank the orange juice one of the crew members had given him, and I was trying to slow my breathing as I let myself feel the fear that had coursed through my body when the man charged toward me. One thing I had learned as a mother is that I always am going to be sure my son is okay first, but that doesn't mean that I don't have to then take care of myself. Saw was okay, and now it was time to be sure I was.

Santiago ruffled Sawyer's hair and then came to sit next to me on the front stoop of the porch where I had slid so I could be near my son but also avoid falling over. "You okay?" he asked.

I nodded. "Yeah, but this is getting a little intense, Santi. I mean twice in a few days."

Santiago pulled me against his side. "Who was it this time?" Saul had called him while I helped get Sawyer settled, but I wasn't sure exactly what he'd said on the call.

"I have no earthly clue. He just said I didn't know what I was doing and tried to touch me." I shivered at the thought of the man straining against my arms.

"Did he touch you? I mean did he hurt you or assault you in any way?" Santiago pulled me back so he could look in my face.

"No, I was able to keep him away from me, but if Saul and his crew members hadn't been here, it might have been a different story," I said quietly as I glanced over at Sawyer. "If he had hurt me with Saw watching . . ." I couldn't even finish the thought.

Santiago pulled me close again. "I'm glad Saul was able to get rid of him, but still, that shouldn't have happened to you."

I sat forward on my own this time and turned back to face him. "Saul didn't get rid of him." I thought a minute about the encounter. "I think he left because he saw how upset Sawyer was."

Santiago frowned. "Really?"

"Yeah, I mean, I think he was about to cry because he'd upset him." Sawyer was grinning at something on his screen, and I gave thanks again for childhood resilience. "He asked if Sawyer was my son, and when I said yes, he apologized." It had been very weird, and from the furrow in his brow, I could tell Santiago thought so, too.

He hugged me again and then stood up. "I'll take you guys home in a bit, but I need to collect statements from Saul and the crew. You okay for a bit?"

"Totally. I'll gather my things, and we'll be ready to go when you are." After he walked toward Saul's office, I slipped inside, grabbed my messenger bag, and made sure all the windows on the shop were locked. I knew Saul had cameras on the lot, and he was diligent about locking the gate. But the last few days had jangled my nerves, and I wasn't exactly feeling very secure in my own body, much less my shop.

Santiago wasn't gone long, and when he came back, he scooped up Sawyer without disrupting the video of Handy Andy putting out the gas station fire and loaded him into the backseat of our car. I slid Beauregard and his basket next to my son, and when he cracked one eye of disdain at me, I rubbed his chin until he purred.

As I headed toward the driver's side door, Santiago put out his hand. "Keys please." I stared at him for a minute, looked over at his cruiser, and then looked back at him. "Savannah and a dispatcher are on their way to get it. I'm on protection duty." He grinned.

"Oh, I see, so now spending time with me is work?" I winked at him.

"Never. Now, work gets even more awesome because I'm spending time with my favorite people." He climbed in and watched as I latched my own seatbelt. "Home?"

"Yes, please," I said as I let myself sink back into the seat. "I kind of just want to be in my space now."

Without another word, Santiago started the car and drove us home. When we got there, he helped me unload both boy and cat, and then he led me to the couch, told me to lay down, and put a blanket over me before saying to Sawyer, "We're going to take care of your mama today, okay? Want to help me with lunch?"

Sawyer looked at me, smiled, and then said, "Yes, I need a sharp knife."

I rolled my eyes and then let them close. A few minutes later, Saw appeared at my side with a grilled cheese sandwich and a bunch of grapes. "Sit up, Mama. You can't eat laying down."

"You're right I can't," I said with a smile at the way Sawyer had just given my own instructions back to me. "This looks delicious. Thank you."

"You can eat here because you're not feeling well," Saw said.

"Thank you so much. I appreciate the chance to rest while I eat." I took a bite of the grilled cheese and almost groaned. Santiago had put both avocado and mushrooms on it, and it was delicious. "Will you go tell Santiago thank you for me?"

"You're most welcome," Santi said as he set Sawyer's plate with two star-shaped sandwiches and grapes on the trunk in front of the couch and then plopped down beside me with his own meal. "Now, what are we going to watch?"

I looked at him out of the corner of my eye. "Really, you don't have to get back to work?"

"This is work, Paisley. Savannah recognized the description given in the statements. It was Landon Farrow at your shop today. Until we know more about what's going on, I'm not leaving your side." He picked up the remote. "What do you say to *Luca?*" he asked Saw.

Sawyer nodded with his mouth full of grilled cheese, and we all tucked into our food and enjoyed the movie. After we ate, Sawyer and Santiago cleaned up, and then Santi convinced Sawyer I needed a nap while they went outside to play on Saw's playground. I don't know how he did it, but Sawyer went willingly and I was asleep in moments.

When I woke up, the room was significantly darker, and I realized I had just slept for several hours. I could hear the boys upstairs, and Sawyer was laughing. I stretched and tried to sit up but was quickly hit with a piercing pain in my feet as Beauregard dug his claws into my flesh to try to keep me from moving.

I shoved him over into the corner and extricated my feet from the blanket before I bled further. Then, I sneaked up the steps and watched from the doorframe while Santiago and Sawyer drove vehicles in and out of the fort they'd made from Saw's covers. They looked so happy together, and I felt a deeper pang of joy than I'd felt in a long time ring through my chest.

I watched and savored the moment before Santiago looked up and caught me watching. I put my finger to my lips and slipped into my room next door to put away some laundry and let them keep playing. In no way did I want to disrupt those special moments.

We spent the rest of the day playing, tidying up the house (mostly after playing), and enjoying time as the three of us. When I took Sawyer up to bed, he was grinning ear to ear. "That was fun, Mama," he said. "I like when Santi comes over."

I smiled. "Me, too, buddy. Me, too. Now what will it be, *Henny* the chicken with arms or *Where The Wild Things Are?*"

"Chickens don't have arms," he said with a laugh.

"Oh this one does," I said as I opened the book and stretched out on my bed next to him. "See?"

Sawyer was asleep before I finished reading about Henny's arm dilemma, and when I went downstairs, I found Santiago asleep with his head on the back of the couch. I slid his shoes off and then lifted his feet onto my lap as he settled onto his back. After a light foot rub, I let him doze further and grabbed my sewing. I was ready, after my extended nap, to tackle Father Winter's face. Faces were often my least favorite part of any project because one misplaced rosy cheek or eye stitch made a Picasso-like figure instead of the mysteriously stern but kind expression I was trying to achieve.

While I counted and recounted and then carefully stitched, I thought about Landon Farrow and why exactly he thought he needed to threaten me. Clearly, he imagined me as some sort of muckraker with an agenda, and I guess if I tried really hard, I could see his point of view on that. But really, I was thrown into this whole situation against my will. I was just doing my job.

Still, I was very puzzled by his reaction to Sawyer's cries. Something had really struck him about a child in pain, and the inquisitive spirit inside me really wanted to look into that. I realized, even in that moment, that looking into his reaction was the exact opposite of what he wanted me to do, but something told me I still needed to puzzle that out. And I could only think of one way to do that.

13

How I convinced Santiago that Mika and I would be completely safe on a little expedition up the hollow to Farrow's house, I'm not sure, especially given how Landon had asked no one to come visit. But when I told my boyfriend I felt like I needed to talk to Landon further and why, he didn't try too hard to stop me.

He did insist, however, that I not go alone, that I keep an open line with Savannah the entire time, and that she wait at the gas station at the bottom of the mountain just in case we needed her. I didn't mind any of these options because despite the previous success Mika and I had in sleuthing, we both knew how quickly a situation could go sideways.

When I said that to Santiago, he laughed. "I think you just like to use the expression *go sideways*." He wasn't wrong.

So Santiago and Sawyer headed toward the playground in the county park as soon as Mika and Savannah arrived at my house. The three of us caravanned in two cars over the mountain and down to the hollow opening, and when Savannah asked us to wait just a minute before going up so that she could

get a coffee and a sweet roll inside, Mika and I decided
Savannah was brilliant and followed her in.

This place was what many rural gas stations had become
now, convenience stores that sold food, basic groceries,
camping supplies, and fuel. Thus, it wasn't surprising to find
the store and the few tables by the deli counter occupied.

What was surprising was that Landon Farrow was sitting at
one of those tables and trying to avoid eye contact with me. I
was a bit flustered when I saw him, but I decided to go on about
my business while also frantically texting Mika and Savannah
to let them know he was here.

Apparently, Landon had told the older man he was with
who I was, too, because when I turned back toward the store
from the counter, the man was standing off to the side and
waiting for me. "Ms. Sutton," he said.

Out of the corner of my eye, I saw Mika and Savannah head
to the only open table in the space and then quietly shift their
chairs so they could both see me. "Yes?" I answered with as big
a smile as I could muster, careful to keep my eyes from drifting
toward Landon who was still seated a few feet behind him.

"I'm Luke Farrow," the man said as he extended a hand. "I
understand you found my father's body."

I swallowed hard and pushed all thoughts of solving a
murder, two murders really, out of my mind and focused,
instead, on a vision of this man as a teenage boy whose father
had been killed. "I did," I said softly. "We did, actually," I
gestured generally toward Mika behind him. "I'm so sorry for
whatever pain that discovery might have caused you." I meant
what I said. I couldn't imagine in any way what that must have
felt like for him.

"Thank you," he said. "Landon here tells me that you have a
little boy."

I smiled reflexively. "I do. He's three and the most amazing
person in the whole world."

Luke smiled. "That's exactly how parents are supposed to feel about their children." He looked back at Landon. "Care to join us?"

A quick glance at my friends confirmed that they were still close by, and I could see Savannah on the phone, probably with Santiago. I was as safe as I was going to get and probably far safer than I would have been at the Farrow house. "Sure," I said, "as long as you won't be offended if I eat this sweet roll before it gets cold."

"I'd be offended if you didn't," Luke said and then held out his elbow so I could take his arm for the five short steps to the table. I wasn't sure if he was being gentlemanly or if he needed my help to steady him as he walked, but either way, we supported each other as we approached the table where Landon had added another chair.

He still wasn't meeting my eyes, but he did smile toward the table when I sat down. "Paisley," he said.

"Landon, it's good to see you again and to meet your grand-father." I smiled over at the old man, who still looked quite nervous but was smiling.

"I'm sorry about yesterday. I lost my temper." He looked up and met my gaze. "I behaved poorly."

"Apology accepted," I said as I noted the slight creases around his eyes and the way his blonde hair was thinning just a little. He looked to be about my age, maybe a little younger, and I had to keep myself from trying to do genealogical math while we talked. "What had you so upset, though, if I may ask?"

The two men looked at each other, and then, Luke turned back to me. "Landon was simply trying to protect the memory of his great-grandmother."

I moved my eyes from Luke to Landon in confusion. "Your great-grandmother? Eleanor? I'm sorry. I don't understand."

Luke sighed. "My mother killed my father, Ms. Sutton."

I puffed up my cheeks as I tried to get my footing at that revelation. I didn't quite know what to say, so I simply nodded.

"He hit her all the time, hit me, too. She was defending herself." Luke said as he looked at his hands.

My mind was spinning with all the implications this revelation had for the past few days, but I forced myself to stay focused on this moment. "Do you want to tell me what happened?" I flicked my eyes from Luke to Landon, who gave me a small nod.

"First," Luke said as he put a grizzled hand on mine, "let me apologize to you and the sheriff for not sharing this information earlier. I've been keeping this secret for eight decades, and once something has been sealed up tight for that long, it's hard to let it out. That's not an excuse, but simply the truth."

I nodded. I had no idea what it was to need to protect my mother, especially in that day and age, from a murder charge that was actually a case of self-defense, and I certainly wasn't going to judge Eleanor Farrow now, a lifetime later. "Of course. It would help, I think, if I knew the story. Then, either you can tell the sheriff or I can, but he'll want to talk to you, I'm sure."

"We were on our way there when you came in," Landon said, "but it seemed like maybe we were supposed to tell you first since you were here and all."

I smiled. "I was actually on my way to your house to talk to you about yesterday." I was still very curious about why Landon had backed off so quickly when Sawyer was upset, but I thought maybe I could start to see the beginning of why. "But I'm glad we met here. I didn't want you to feel ambushed."

Luke laughed. "Never you worry about that, Ms. Sutton. It's the neighbors further up the hollow that have the 'shoot on sight' signs."

I'd seen those signs, and despite Luke's light tone, he and I both knew his neighbors would shoot first and ask questions later if they felt it necessary. "That is much appreciated."

"It was bad that night, really bad," Luke began without further prompting. "Daddy had been drinking and railing about how the government was trying to destroy him and his family by sending him away. He kept talking about how the Confederates and the Union soldiers had done the same thing to his grandfather, and they'd lost all of the farm but the land we lived on." Luke sighed. "He was so angry."

I nodded and thought about all the stories I'd read of Confederate soldiers who were conscripted into a war they didn't want to fight, about how they didn't care about the "Southern Cause" because they had never been wealthy enough to enslave anyone. I had always thought that ironic given how many of the people who proudly sported Confederate flags nowadays wouldn't have been getting any of the "benefits" of slavery back then anyway. It was a weird thing.

"So he just kept dodging. Refusing to show up to draft days. Missing his appointments for his physical over and over again. And when the police came, he'd make Mama lie for him and say he was in town, when really he was just up in the hayloft hiding." Luke shook his head.

"I'm not a supporter of most wars myself. Saw what that kind of battle can do to a person, but Daddy was putting all of us into trouble. Add to that his drinking and his fists. . . and well, life was right miserable about then."

"Sounds awful," I said with conviction, because it did. I glanced over at Landon, who had both hands wrapped around his coffee mug and was staring into it like it was a wishing well. "Do you want to tell me about the day he died?"

Landon looked up at his grandfather, and I could see the anxiety in his eyes. I quickly added, "You don't have to, not at all. Sheriff Shifflett needs to know far more than I do if it's too painful to share twice or if you'd rather not talk with me about it. I completely understand."

Luke reached over and took his grandson's hand and then

he looked at me. "I want you to know, so that you understand why Landon came to see you yesterday." He sighed, "And because I understand your father and his friends have made the ultimate choice to protect my mother."

I swallowed hard as tears burned my eyes. I had been trying not to think about Dad, trying not to put all this together, but now, there it was. My dad had been protecting someone else, someone who didn't deserve to be charged with murder or even to have her name maligned after the fact. And Homer had been doing the same without knowing it. But both Ace and Melvin were willing to risk their freedom to protect this woman.

They were willing to risk their freedom to protect this woman. I couldn't think about it too much, though, or I'd be sobbing into my sweet roll. So I took a bite instead and just nodded.

"My father was very angry that night, still seething from some encounter at the bar a few days before, and Mom was tired. That's all I can think because if she wasn't tired, she would have realized Dad was on edge. Instead, she asked him to help her lift the couch so she could sweep under it." Luke's face got a far off look, and I saw his hands clench the table.

Landon sighed just as I groaned.

"He went after her with the knife, claimed she didn't realize how hard he worked, that it was her job to keep the house clean, not his, and what did she do all day anyway?" Luke's voice was kind of monotone.

I tried to imagine the scene – a small farmstead with a garden and probably chickens, maybe a cow. A child to take care of, meals to cook, and a violent husband. Eleanor's days must have been frantic. But I'd heard other women talk about how their husbands said something similar, as if being at home didn't require the same kind of effort or work that a job elsewhere did.

"Fortunately, Dad had been drinking," Luke continued,

"and he stumbled. Mom grabbed the knife when he dropped it, and when he lunged at her, she held it out." Luke looked at Landon. "She wasn't angry. She wasn't even scared, I don't think. She was just so very tired."

A silence settled around us for a few moments, and I sat with the scene. A woman simply defending herself, almost passively so, but then the ramifications for that simple act becoming huge if something wasn't done. I was anxious just thinking about it.

"I called one of the men from church, told him what had happened, and he walked me through what I needed to do," Luke said. "They'd always been trying to help Mom and me out, but Dad was so prideful. That night, though, I needed him."

I thought I knew where the story went from here. "And the next day they came and helped you get rid of the body?"

Luke met my eyes. "Exactly. So you see, they had nothing to do with it. If anything, I should be charged."

I shook my head. "You were a child. Santiago will sort this out, and you're doing the right thing to talk to him." I leaned forward. "Thank you for sharing that with me."

Landon stood up. "So when your son got upset yesterday . . ." he didn't finish.

"I completely get it, and I completely get you wanting to protect your family," I said as I stood up beside him. "Maybe next time, though, just try talking to me instead of threatening me, okay?"

Landon sighed. "I'm sorry."

I nodded and helped Luke to his feet. "Would you like me to let Santiago know you're on your way? He's not at the office, but he can meet you there."

"That would be great, and if it's not too much to ask," Landon said, "I'd love to meet your son sometime. Apologize to him for getting him upset even indirectly."

"No apology is needed, but he'll be with the sheriff. Maybe we can all go that way, and then you can meet him." I wasn't sure how Sawyer would react to seeing Landon again, but I knew that it was better for him to confront his fear in a safe way than to randomly see Landon out and about and not really know what to do. We lived in a small place after all.

The men got into Landon's car, and Savannah, Mika, and I made our way back to town, too, with Savannah on speaker so I could fill her and Mika in on what had happened while we drove. "I'm so angry," I said after I told them about Leo Farrow's death. "He terrorized his wife and child, and his abuse has lingered in this family for generations."

Mika sighed. "And we brought it all out into the light."

"But light is what heals. Always. Secrets never heal." Savannah's voice was firm and clear, and I knew she was right.

WHEN WE ARRIVED at the station, Santiago and Sawyer were out front walking across the planters by the sidewalk like they were balance beams. Santiago had headed right over as soon as I'd texted him, and while I knew that he had a lot more on his mind than entertaining my son, I appreciated that he was keeping Saw busy until I got there. I also appreciated his balancing ability. It was almost as impressive as Sawyer's.

When the Farrows walked over, Sawyer hid behind my legs but smiled. Landon bent down and said, "Sawyer, I owe your mommy an apology for getting loud with her before, and I wanted to say I'm sorry to you, too. I'm so sorry I scared you."

Sawyer, with the resilience of a child, reached up, took my hand, and said, clear as day, "It's okay" and went right back to walking the wall behind us.

Santiago stepped down and walked with the Farrows inside, leaving the rest of us to stand on the sidewalk and wonder what to do. Fortunately, Sawyer, when around people he knew, was never short of words or ideas, so he babbled on a bit about how he climbed the firefighter's pole at the playground and then said he was hungry for tacos.

"Ooh, there's a new food truck here, heard it's a spinoff of one over on the shore of Maryland. Their mole is supposed to be amazing," Savannah said. "My treat."

Sawyer jumped up and down and then took Savannah's hand as they walked up and around the corner toward the courthouse, where the black truck with the words "Lu Two" on the side was parked. If the scents coming from the vent at the top of the truck were any indication, these were going to be some amazing tacos.

And they were. So amazing, in fact, that Sawyer ate two chicken tacos himself, which for the boy who regularly hates everything from lollipops to chicken nuggets was an amazing feat. I ate three myself, so I also know of which I speak.

We had scarfed down our food at the picnic table tucked beside the police station, and now, we were a bit aimless again, not sure whether to head out or wait until Santiago came to tell us what was next for Luke Farrow and for my dad and his friends. I was just about to suggest that we head to Mika's shop so that Savannah could get back to work when Dad walked over.

"Santiago asked me to come down," he said when I stood up in surprise. "Asked us all to come down."

I looked over Dad's shoulder and saw Ace, Melvin, and Homer walking toward us. "Oh, okay. Did he tell you why?" I didn't want to give anything away if Santiago had some plan for how the conversation would go with the men.

"Said Luke and Landon are inside, that Luke told them about Eleanor, and he just needed our corroborating statements so that this could all be put to bed." Dad smiled, but I could tell his heart wasn't in it. This whole situation had put a strain on him, and I knew that it would take a while for him to recover fully. Stress gets harder to bear as we age, at least it does for me.

"Well, that's good," I said. "Want some moral support?"

"I'd love that," Dad said as he scooped Sawyer up into a big bear hug. "Keep me company, Saw-guy?"

"Sure . . . but first, I need another taco," Sawyer said as he squirmed out of Dad's arm and sprinted up the street toward the taco truck.

Dad started after him, but I put an arm on dad's and took off after my kid. Neither of us was going to catch the boy, but I had a better chance than Dad at this point. Sawyer turned the corner toward the courthouse, and just as he did, a car jumped up onto the sidewalk and gunned its engine.

Something supernatural kicked in, and I leaped forward just in time to push Sawyer into a doorway alcove. I pressed him against the door and put my body in front of him. But I didn't feel an impact or even a breeze. When I looked out, the car was speeding up the block with Savannah staring after it, her phone to her mouth. Someone had tried to kill my son.

FORTUNATELY, Sawyer was oblivious to the intention behind the car and thought someone had just been "tracted" by their phone or something, but I had seen how the car's wheels had veered up and onto that curb just in front of where Sawyer was running. Whoever had been driving that car aimed for my little boy, and now, I was gunning for them.

As Sawyer ate another taco and I tried to keep mine in my stomach, Santiago rushed over to where we were sitting on the grass, far back from the road, in front of the station. "Savannah got the plate. Are you two okay?" He was a bit breathless, but I could tell he was controlling his response so as not to scare Sawyer.

I nodded. "We're fine. Sawyer is, apparently, great," I said as I stared at him eating the last bite of his third taco.

"And you?" Santiago whispered as he helped me up from the grass.

"I may need to get a heartrate monitor if this kind of thing keeps happening, but yeah, I'm okay," I said as I buried my face in his neck for a second. "They were aiming for Sawyer, Santi." I choked back a sob.

"I know. We're going to get them, Pais." He pulled away from me and looked into my face. "But for now, let's get you inside." He turned toward Sawyer. "Savannah has set up an obstacle course through the building, Saw. Think you're up to the challenge?"

As Sawyer stood and prepared to bolt toward the building, Santi grabbed him around the waist and threw him over his shoulder. "Oh no you don't. The first obstacle is for you to manage to hold on while I run you like a sack of potatoes."

The two of them took off toward the building, and only then did I realize that Mika, my dad, Ace, Homer, and Melvin were standing nearby. "Care for an entourage?" Mika asked as she slipped her arm around my waist.

I leaned against her and said, "I couldn't imagine a better gaggle of groupies than you guys." I smiled, and the men all nodded and followed us into the building.

14

The afternoon was, thankfully, uneventful. Santiago got everyone's statements, wrote up his report, and then invited the local reporter to come over and get an exclusive about Leo Farrow's death. He was forthright with the facts about Farrow's behavior, but he also didn't disparage the dead. His most important intention in the interview was to make it clear that given that Eleanor Farrow had acted in self-defense, she would not, by today's standard, be charged with murder.

The commonwealth's attorney had already sent the reporter a written statement corroborating that fact and also establishing that the statute of limitations for unlawful disposal of a body, the crime which Ace and Melvin would have been charged with, was long past, so no charges would be pressed in the case of Leo Farrow's death.

The only thing I still couldn't figure out is why Summer had gotten so squirrely. Santiago had called her to ask her to come in and make a formal statement for the file, but she had flat-out refused. Said she wanted nothing further to do with this case or with me. Some day, I was going to look into that, but today, I had enough to manage.

Lucille and Dad had joined Mika, Sawyer, Savannah, and me at Mika's shop so that we could all be together and prep for my grand opening. For a fleeting moment, I had thought about postponing the opening, but given all the advertising I'd done, the fact that most everything was in place already, and the fact that I thought we could all use the distraction, I kept to my original plan and let Lucille do her thing and build the day into a baked-good infused celebration.

By the time Santiago came to pick up Sawyer and me, Lucille already had plans to make rugelach, orange pound cake, fudge, and no-bake cookies to give out to customers. In between helping customers, Mrs. Stephenson had suggested she bring over some sweet tea and 7-Up punch, and Dad had decided – in a fit of strange relief, I suppose – to get out an old gorilla suit he had used for Halloween when I was a kid and stand on the road waving to get people's attention.

Now my grand opening was beginning to resemble a fall festival mixed with a tax service ad campaign, and I was thrilled. I couldn't quite get the image of the car charging toward my little boy out of my head, but the plans were helping distract me. For that, I was grateful.

Still, when Santiago got Sawyer buckled into his seat, and I had buckled into mine, I sort of caved in a little. The stress of the past few days was weighing heavy on me, and I couldn't begin to be more thankful that Santiago was coming home with us. Dad and Lucille and Mika had all offered to come over and help with any last minute prep, but I honestly couldn't think of anything that needed to be done. Plus, I really just wanted a quiet night with my two guys.

When we got home, I made us scrambled egg sandwiches while Santiago and Sawyer built an epic sand castle under the playground. Then, after we ate, we all jogged around in the yard chasing Beauregard for a bit because he had stolen Saw's stuffed crow and was carrying it around like he was a prime hunter.

All four of us, apparently, enjoyed the game because when Sawyer finally managed to grab Beau and extricate the bird from his mouth, the cat settled into Sawyer's arms and began to purr. Then, when it was time for bed after a bath, the boy, the bird, and the Beau all climbed under the covers and were asleep almost instantly. At least I think the crow was asleep.

Back downstairs, Santiago and I each had a beer, and I turned on my newest favorite show, *Mythic Quest*. I just loved the quirky writing and the strange characters, and a video game production studio was so far from my life in every way that it was the perfect escape.

Unfortunately, I was sound asleep with my head in Santiago's lap midway through the first episode, but when he helped me climb the stairs, waited outside while I changed into my pj's, and then came to tuck me into bed, I felt like maybe I might just doze off on the couch more often.

THE NEXT MORNING, I woke at five a.m., the excitement of opening my very own store so big in my mind that I couldn't get back to sleep. I slid out of bed, being sure not to even shift Sawyer's tiny body beside me, and slipped down the stairs past where I could hear Santiago snoring in Sawyer's room. Only Beauregard stirred and padded down the stairs after me. I guess he'd had enough being snuggled by a toddler for a while.

In the kitchen, I ground enough coffee beans for two French presses full, and I lined up a tray of cheese toast to slip in when I heard the guys stirring upstairs. Then, mug of coffee in hand, I slipped out into the dawn morning and took a deep breath. It was still pretty humid out, but I could feel the first hints of crispness in the air. Autumn would be here soon, and I was going to treasure every last hot day because it meant I'd appreciate the cool ones even more when they came.

Down the hill a bit, I could hear a woodpecker tapping away, and back behind the house, a barn owl cried. It was the cusp between night and day, and somehow, it felt perfect to be out in it on this hugely important day in my life.

Still, I couldn't shake the memory of that car careening toward Sawyer, and I wondered what Savannah had found about the plate. I hadn't asked yesterday because I knew that she and Santiago had the situation in hand, and I wanted to shift my focus away from the case and toward my grand opening. But now, here in the dark quiet of dawn, I was curious.

I needed to focus, though, so I pushed the image out of my mind and, instead, envisioned a crowd of people around my little store-shed talking and browsing and munching on Lucille's baked goods. It was an image that kept me smiling and dreaming until I heard the reverberation of little footfalls through the walls of the house and headed in to greet my little boy.

I DEFINITELY WANTED Sawyer to be a part of the grand opening, but I knew he wouldn't tolerate a whole day of hanging out at the shop. His dad was coming to get him at noon so they could spend a little extra time together, and I could focus on my shop during the hours when things would probably be the most busy in the afternoon.

When Santiago, Sawyer, and I pulled up to the lot, I laughed out loud. Saul and his crew had decorated all their heavy equipment with lights and mums and then parked them along the street so that everyone driving by would definitely see that something big was going on. As I got out of the car, I saw my dad and step-mom, Mika, Savannah, and every member of Saul's crew, including Saul, moving around the lot to water plants, pull reappearing weeds, and tidy up any random corner of mess. It was so unexpected and so very beautiful.

At the shop itself, everything was open, the coffee was brewing, and Lucille had set up a beautiful display of baked goods with a sign that said, "In Appreciation of Our Customers." It was a brilliant idea because we all know that sometimes when someone gives you something for free, you're more inclined to spend. Plus, I really did want to show appreciation to anyone who came by.

The opening was set to begin at ten a.m., but at just before nine, the first customers starting coming in, lured – I imagined – by the glowing backhoes and dump trucks. Soon, the crowd was substantial, and it seemed like the more cars were in the lot, the more came. Word was definitely spreading, and when the local news van showed up to ask if they could interview me for a piece on the Mid-Day show, I was thrilled.

I did the brief interview and told them to film anything they wished. Then, I spent the rest of the morning greeting customers, answering questions about my merchandise, and giving out my card to people who were considering bringing me in for a salvage job. When Sawyer's dad arrived at noon, I barely had time to give my boy a big hug, fill his dad in on the car incident from the day before, and promise to keep him posted on the investigation. He was far from thrilled with the situation, of course, but he seemed to understand that I was pretty shaken, too, and that might have been the best I could hope for given the circumstances.

The afternoon was even busier than the morning, and by four o'clock, the entire lot was filled with cars, some with out-of-state plates, and somehow, Saul had even brought in a local band to play from the back of one of the trucks. My grand opening had become a county event, and I loved it.

I loved, even more, that people were buying things. Bottles were selling, and a couple had bought a lovely set of old doors that I'd pulled from the parish house at Bethel Church. Mika's knitted goods were moving, too, and Dad spent considerable time talking with one man about Ace's old plow.

The plan had been to shut everything up at five p.m. so that we could prepare for the next day's sales, but the crowd was still flowing in at four forty-five. Saul suggested we stay open until seven and see how it went. I agreed given that word of mouth was the best advertisement in these parts, and there were a lot of mouths here.

Sales kept coming, and people kept eating Lucille's baked goods. On Mika's suggestion, she'd put out a tip jar, and with the proceeds she collected there, she promised to make me a whole new set of deliciousness for the next day. I wondered if this event might be just the way to get Lucille to start that baking business she was always half-joking about.

Santiago and Savannah stayed low-key for the day. Savannah was in uniform, since she was technically on duty, but she mostly hung out by her cruiser and just kept a steady presence. Santiago, however, patrolled regularly, looking, I expected, for the person who had tried to kill my son.

We still hadn't talked about who that might be because there hadn't been a chance to do so. I had thought about asking Santiago when I got a chance, but I figured it was better I keep my focus on my store and let him do the police stuff. I had no doubt he was almost as eager as I was to find the person who had tried to hurt Saw.

Seven p.m. rolled around, and the crowd had begun to thin. Just a few cars were left in the lot, and most people had begun to head home as the sun dipped into the trees. That was just as well since Saul's lot was not lit, and none of us wanted the liability if someone got hurt in the dark.

When the last of the customers had pulled out, Saul and his crew, who had stayed all day to support me, began to help us pack up the things that needed to be moved into my shop. We had decided to leave the lights on to draw people in for tomorrow, and Saul hoped that the extra light would help deter anyone from trying to sneak in. Just for the sake of security, though, he was going to install an extra lock on the gate to accompany the "This Property Is Under Video Surveillance" signs he'd hung on the fence throughout the day. We both knew that more attention meant more of the unwanted kind, too.

Everyone but Santiago and I headed out for the night, and while some of Saul's crew said they'd come back to help tomorrow, I made them promise to enjoy their weekends and stay home. They had already done so much for me, Saul especially, and I didn't want them feeling beholden to me or my business. From the half-hearted nods they gave me, I expected I'd see some of them tomorrow anyway.

As Santiago and I locked up, I took a minute to stand back and look at my shop. It was glowing in the light of the Edison bulbs, and I could see the shimmer of the items inside reflecting through the windows. It was beautiful.

Santiago slid up next to me and pulled me into his side. "This is amazing, Pais," he said quietly.

"Isn't it, though?" I whispered before turning to him. "Thank you for all your help."

He leaned forward and kissed me, and then he took a step back and knelt down. I stared at him for a second, but then the sound of car tires on the gravel grabbed my attention.

I looked up just in time to see headlights barreling toward us. I dove for Santiago, and we rolled out of the way and into the shadow of my shop just before the car reached us. I had barely taken a breath when Santiago whispered, "Stay in the shadows and close to the building."

He had his phone out and said, "Savannah, she's here. She must have given you the slip. Send back-up." As he and I crawled toward the door of my shop, I heard the engine rev behind the building. The car was coming to take another pass.

I scrambled up onto the porch as I tried to fumble the keys from my pocket. The headlights started to come around the corner, and both Santiago and I dove to the other side of the porch away from the lights. The beams skimmed up the side of the building as the car took the corner toward us. I shimmied my way under the porch and felt Santiago slide in beside me as the car came around past where we'd both been laying.

"Now what?" I shouted as the tires skidded on the gravel in another circle around the building.

"Now we stay put," Santiago said.

I groaned as I tried to take a full breath and felt the braces of the porch press against my back. I had a fleeting image of a hound dog under a log cabin.

"Savannah will be here shortly, and I expect she'll bring the cavalry." Santiago wiggled closer to me and pressed his hand down on mine.

Just then, I heard the door of a car close, and then a voice that felt a little familiar sang, "I know you're here, Paisley Sutton. Don't think my car is the only way I can get rid of you."

I felt Santiago's hand slide down to his gun, and I felt comforted that he was with me. But I didn't want him to do anything sudden, especially since it seemed like maybe the driver didn't know where we were.

"You just don't have the loyalty to family that I do. Do you? You keep riling things up in some quest for the truth. When really the only thing that matters is that we take care of our own." I could hear her footsteps getting closer as she came up along the side of my shop.

"My uncle didn't deserve this, Paisley. He didn't deserve to have his name dragged through the mud by the likes of you. He was a good man, a man who tried to help, and you couldn't let it rest." Her footfalls sounded heavy now on the porch above us. The doorknob of the shop rattled, and as she stepped closer, I thought I saw her lean in and look through the windows.

"But since you couldn't leave well enough alone, I'm just going to have to shut you up. Shouldn't be hard once you're dead to convince everyone that you just brought up this story to get attention for your business." She stepped back off the porch, and I could have reached out and touched the back of her booties.

"Good thing," she dropped to her knees and shone the flashlight in my eyes, "that I found you then." California Davis-Baca reached under the porch and grabbed me by the hand as she tried to tug me out of the porch where I was wedged.

I stuck my left hand up against the rafters and pulled back. She might dislocate my elbow, but I was not going to let her get me out in the open where she could kill me more easily.

She had managed to drag me a couple of feet forward since she had the leverage of her legs, and I only had one twisted arm flung up above me. My head was almost to the edge of the porch, and I was ready to fling my free arm over my face to protect myself. But then, California tumbled away from me across the yard.

"Stay where you are, Pais," Santiago said, somehow above me. He jumped off the porch and grabbed California's arms before handcuffing her wrists behind her back and standing her up. "Okay, now you can come out."

"Um, no I can't," I said as I realized that I was wholly and completely stuck under the porch of my own salvage store. "I'm going to need some help."

A FEW MOMENTS LATER, Savannah, Saul, and three members of his crew pulled up like the cavalry Santiago had claimed, and everyone worked together to lift my shop just a couple of inches so I could shimmy out. It wasn't my most graceful moment, but I was very grateful.

As Savannah drove California Davis-Baca off in her cruiser, I plopped down on the porch of my store. "Well, that was unexpected," I said to everyone gathered around me. "What in the world was she upset with me about?"

"I expect we'll find out, but we've known since this afternoon that she was the one who tried to kill Sawyer. Savannah had her under surveillance, but California gave her the slip a bit ago. That's when she came here." Santiago sat down next to me. "Sorry, Paisley."

I shook my head. "We caught her. That's all that matters, and she made some really incriminating statements in your presence, so that's good, right?"

"That is good," Santiago said, "but given our relationship, I'm probably going to need more than just my word and yours."

"Fortunately, I learned a trick or two from Mika." I held up my phone and flipped to the voice recording I had turned on as soon as I heard the car door. "Will this help?" I pressed play, and California's voice was clear as a bell.

Santiago kissed my cheek. "Of course it will. Good thinking." He helped me to my feet. "Now, let's get you home to bed."

I nodded. "Okay. I want to call Sawyer on the way home," I said.

"Okay, then let me do this." Savannah spit on her fingers and then proceeded to clean all the dirt off my face. "Now Mama doesn't look like she was mud wrestling."

I chuckled. "Thanks."

THE NEXT DAY, California Davis-Baca was charged with the murder of Melvin Smith. She had apparently poisoned his coffee at his store just before he came over to my house that day, and the timing just happened to work out to look like he'd been poisoned by someone at my place. A closer examination, though, revealed he had ingested the poison earlier, and two of his employees at the restaurant testified to seeing California round his car at just about the perfect time in the poisoning timeline.

It turned out that she was worried that Melvin, Ace, Homer, my dad and I would eventually throw her uncle Stephen under the bus since he had already died. She didn't want her family's name tainted that way and had been looking for opportunities to get her revenge on all of us. Savannah filled us in the next morning, but so far, only Melvin had been an easy target. The rest of us were harder to reach, and so she'd decided to start with me since if she killed me, the investigation might not go anywhere at all.

I sighed as Savannah and I sipped our coffee on my shop porch and watched the early bird customers browse around. "How in the world she thought she was going to pull that off and not get caught, I have no idea," Savannah said.

"Well, Eleanor Farrow's family and friends protected her for eighty years. I guess it is possible," I answered as I watched a little girl choose a small stained glass piece from a display I'd put out this morning.

"Yes, but everyone liked Eleanor Farrow. Everyone knew her story. No one had even known California Davis-Baca existed until she turned up here." Savannah sighed. "We joke a lot about newcomers and such here, but we take care of our own."

I nodded and looked around at the growing crowd. "Yes, yes we do." I thought as I got up to ring up the little girl with the stained glass and her dad with five blue bottles for his new bottle tree in his garden. Yes we do.

A FREE COZY SET IN SAN FRANCISCO

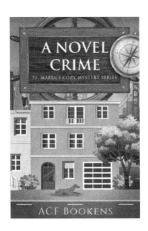

Join my Cozy Up email group for weekly book recs & a FREE copy of *A Novel Crime*, the prequel to the St. Marin's Cozy Mystery Series.
Sign-up here - https://bookens.andilit.com/CozyUp

ABOUT THE AUTHOR

AACF Bookens lives in the Blue Ridge Mountains of Virginia, where the mountain tops remind her that life is a rugged beauty of a beast worthy of our attention. When she's not writing, she enjoys chasing her son around the house with the full awareness she will never catch him, cross-stitching while she binge-watches police procedurals, and reading everything she can get her hands on. Find her at bookens.andilit.com.

ALSO BY ACF BOOKENS

St. Marin's Cozy Mystery Series

Publishable By Death

Entitled To Kill

Bound To Execute

Plotted For Murder

Tome To Tomb

Scripted To Slay

Proof Of Death

Epilogue of An Epitaph

Hardcover Homicide - Coming December 2021

Stitches In Crime Series

Crossed By Death

Bobbins and Bodies

Hanged By A Thread

Counted Corpse

Sewn At The Crime - Coming in January 2022

Manufactured by Amazon.ca
Bolton, ON

24523266R00096